Ocean of Death . . .

I just wanted to get back to the *Amy Denise*, my temporary home, and sleep. I pushed the dinghy into the tide, climbed in, and reached into the bottom for an oar to push off with. My hand grabbed pure air.

"What the . . . ?" Somebody had stolen both oars. The life jackets were gone as well.

I was too tired to cuss or care as I jerked the engine to life. The dinghy puttered faithfully against the choppy tide, until a heavy swell rocked the little boat violently—and the entire engine slid off of the stern into the ocean. Another wave hit the boat broadside, and suddenly I was in the water, gagging and flailing.

The water was very cold, and getting rougher. I treaded water and craned my neck to look for the *Amy Denise*. She was only a dim shape in the night. Determinedly, I struck out against the tide, and with the first overhand stroke, I knew my effort was doomed.

Engines don't just fall off boats, I thought. Somebody had not wanted me to return safely to the *Amy Denise*. Somebody had not wanted me to keep asking questions.

Suddenly I knew who'd committed the murders. And I wouldn't live to tell Geof about it, and the killer would go free . . .

Books by Nancy Pickard

Bum Steer
Dead Crazy
Generous Death
I.O.U.
Marriage Is Murder
No Body
Say No to Murder

Published by POCKET BOOKS

NANCY PICKARD

A JENNY CAIN MYSTERY

SAY NO TO MURDER

POCKET BOOKS

New York   London   Toronto   Sydney   Tokyo   Singapore

POCKET BOOKS, a division of Simon & Schuster Inc.
1230 Avenue of the Americas, New York, NY 10020

Copyright © 1985 by Nancy Pickard

ISBN: 0-671-73431-8

First Pocket Books printing July 1988

10 9 8 7 6 5

POCKET and colophon are registered trademarks of
Simon & Schuster Inc.

Cover illustration by Dan Craig/Oasis Studio

Printed in the U.S.A.

*With love and thanks
to my mother and father*

prologue

You wouldn't believe some of the projects on which people want to spend money. For example, on my desk at the Port Frederick Civic Foundation there is a superbly persuasive piece of begging that appeals for funds to establish a Bilingual Academy of Latin Studies for Local Residents of Mexican-American Descent. A fine and highfalutin notion, right? Except that we are 1,000 miles north of the border, and the only Latino in town is the one who wrote the grant proposal, no other Mexicans ever having been stupid enough to leave that climate for this one. According to the grant application, the "project developer" is presently unemployed, but is willing to accept a sacrifice salary to become director of said academy.

Nay, José.

Then there's the request for the many thousands of dollars it would take to levy and enforce a total trade embargo against the State of New York. *This,* mind you, is the State of Massachusetts.

Application denied.

My assistant director, Derek Jones, particularly likes the application that asks the Foundation to fund the construction of a "small but tasteful" massage parlor, complete with a movie theater for "short, tasteful" porno flicks. All this, one assumes, for a clientele of short but tasteful men.

Close, but no cigarillo.

My favorite, however, is the one that proposes to send a dozen college students to every ski resort in the Adirondacks and the Rockies "in order to ascertain the scientific validity of the claim that it is more difficult to ski on ice than on powder." The applicants—coincidentally a dozen fraternity brothers from the University of Virginia— envision a four-year project with expenses limited to economy airfares, cheap hotels and three-day lift tickets. (Students from more northern schools tend to request funding to study the differences among the sands of Florida beaches. Or was it tans?)

Applications also denied, but with regret.

Actually, we couldn't fund such worthy causes even if we wanted to, which in the case of the massage parlor, Derek does. For one thing, our own charter limits us to charitable activities in Port Frederick, which knocks the skis out from under those enterprising young men from Virginia. And, as a private charitable foundation, we are also regulated—not to say hog-tied—by myriad laws that govern how we may accrue, invest and spend the millions of dollars that various donors have bequeathed over the years to this Foundation.

Most folks don't know all that, however. So we get a constant flow of inappropriate applications from individuals and causes we can't help. And that means that as director of the Foundation, I spend a lot of my time saying "no" to some perfectly nice and deserving people.

And to some perfect jerks.

One of whom appeared at our office that second stifling week of June, screaming holy bloody murder. It was a sadly appropriate and prophetic thing for him to do.

chapter
1

He was seated by my desk waiting for me when I strolled into the office at 7:30 that morning. When I glimpsed him, I raised an accusing eyebrow at my secretary, Faye Basil. Ordinarily, she won't allow strangers into my inner sanctum when I'm away, but has them wait under her watchful eyes instead.

"Morning, Faye." I smiled forgivingly at her. I had awakened in a sunny summer mood which had not even wilted in the face of a day that was hot enough to pop corn.

Faye gulped, which seemed an odd reply.

I continued across the cheap, well-worn carpet to my equally cheaply furnished, well-worn office. (My bosses, the five trustees of the Foundation, occasionally make half-hearted attempts to persuade me to redecorate. I always refuse, to their collective relief, because every cent we spend on administrative expenses is a penny stolen from the charities we support. And that's why our office looks like a home for underprivileged MBAs.) The visitor, hearing my entrance, whirled to stare. Then he stood to face me.

Suddenly, the cause of Faye's uncharacteristic helplessness was startlingly apparent.

He was a force of nature, rising.

The man was enormous, easily six foot nine, with the furious beady eyes of a grizzly. He was like the old joke: Where does a 300-pound gorilla sit? . . . Anywhere he wants.

"Are you Jennifer Cain?" he roared at me.

It was like being stopped dead in one's tracks by a gust of wind. I clung to the edge of Faye's desk for psychic, if not physical, balance.

"Yes, I am."

"Who the hell do you think you are!"

Actually, I thought we'd already established that, but I didn't say so. Instead, I decided the safest course was to consider it a rhetorical question, and I countered, "Who are you?"

"Ansen Reich," he snarled.

"Oh," I said slowly, in the tone with which one might greet an auditor from the IRS. My morning no longer seemed so bright and cheerful. An uneasy silence settled over the office while he let the unpleasant news of his identity sink into my consciousness. Like Faye, I gulped.

Then I tried a placating smile.

"Mr. Reich, please try to . . ."

"You shut up!" The pencils on Faye's desk quivered, as did her lower lip. "I've had it with your lying crap. You're gonna listen to me this time, girl, and you're gonna listen good."

"Now you wait just one minute!" I bellowed back at him, thus bringing to a close the most sensitive and intelligent moments of our interview. "Mr. Reich, I am truly sorry for you and your family, but I am sick of your abusive phone calls . . ."

"Wait a minute?" He lurched toward me so I felt an overwhelming urge to step back. "You want me to wait a minute like my Philly did? Wait a minute, wait an hour, wait four hours? And nobody answers the goddamn telephone at the goddamn suicide center because you haven't paid the goddamn telephone bill . . ."

Faye made an anguished sound.

"Mr. Reich," I protested, "you know that isn't true . . ."

"Don't you dish out that crap no more, lady. That telephone bill didn't get paid on time and you're the stupid broad who didn't pay it. And that's why the phone company shut off service, and that's why my Philly couldn't get help when he needed it, and that's why he strung himself up from those I-beams. And if you think I'm gonna let you forget what this outfit done to my boy, you got another . . ."

"Mr. Reich, be quiet!"

I hadn't known I had the volume in me.

It must have surprised him, too, because he was rendered speechless long enough for me to slide in a few angry words of my own.

"Mr. Reich, I have explained to you that we are not the funding agency for the suicide center. It is located over the town boundary, and we are not allowed to fund anything outside Port Frederick. I have also explained to you more than once that we didn't even know their phone was being cut off until it had already happened, and that we were going to help them if we had to take the money from our own pockets, but that . . ."

"Bull! They told me you didn't get down to the phone company on time . . ."

"Well, no, but . . ."

". . . got all the money in the world for every pissant minority, but you can't spare a few measly bucks to pay a measly phone bill that could of saved the life of one white boy. You're so busy with your precious harbor reconstruction, spending millions on goddamn cutesy cafés when there's young kids killing themselves because they can't get help when they need it. Too busy struttin' around the docks, ain't you, shellin' out dough for paint and crap? Got no money to help my boy! And now he's dead! And I'm telling you girl, I hold you personally responsible . . ."

"That's not fair."

"Tell it to the judge, girl."

"Does that mean you're going to sue us, Mr. Reich?" If he called me girl, lady or broad one more time, I was going to knock off his top nine inches. Sure I was. "On what grounds, exactly?"

"Sue you?" He cracked an ugly grin. "Hell no, I don't have the money for that, and you know it. You got the big-buck lawyers, not me." His grin grew wider and uglier. "But I got something else that's important to you, don't I? I got some power you can't fight, girl."

"I don't know what you're talking about."

He laughed, in a manner of speaking.

"Don't you? Well, you come on down to the docks tomorrow, lady. You just mosey on down to your precious groundbreaking ceremony!"

"What?" I was bewildered by his references to Liberty Harbor, the waterfront renovation on which the Foundation had sunk several hundred thousand dollars and the town had sunk its hopes for economic revival. Bewildered, and suddenly nervous.

He shoved past me and thundered out the door before I got my wits sufficiently together to press him for answers.

"Oh, Jenny," Faye whispered. She was near tears. At fifty, and widowed for five years with three teenage boys to support, Faye still found time and heart enough to volunteer one night a week at the suicide center which the sixteen-year-old Reich boy had not been able to reach the night he killed himself. It was she who'd immediately directed the center to me for emergency aid when she learned of their fiscal crisis. She said shakily, "If only I'd known sooner, maybe we could have saved that child."

"It's not your fault," I said gently, and took one of her hands to pat. With my free hand, I thumbed through her Rolodex for a mobile phone number and, on a hunch, dialed it.

"Shattuck!" the builder and general contractor at Liberty Harbor shouted into the phone in his Cadillac, over the din of construction at the waterfront. Official groundbreaking might still be one day away, but work had begun a month ago.

"Goose!" I yelled back at him, so that Faye looked up, startled. "It's Jenny Cain."

"I remember you! Tall, blond, beautiful, missing!"

"All right." I smiled. "I've been busy."

"So tell him you have other fish to fry," said my favorite sixty-year-old unregenerate flirt. "I, for one, heat up nice and tasty."

"I'll bet you do, since you certainly are fresh as they come."

He chuckled. "What can I do for you, Miss Jenny?"

"Do you have a man by the name of Reich working for you?"

"Sure! Little squirt, about five-two?"

"That's the one." My heart began to sink even before Goose tied the final rock to it. "What's he do for you?"

"Construction foreman."

"Oh." It was worse than I thought. I knew all too well that a good foreman could bring a job in under deadline, on budget; while a bad foreman could . . . "What's the word on him, Goose?"

"World-class jackass," he informed me in his own inimitable style, "but a hell of a fine foreman, in his way. Why?"

"I understand his son committed suicide a couple of days ago . . ." Beside me, Faye blew her nose; I gave her hand another pat.

"Right." Goose lowered the boom of his voice a moment. "Poor guy's been goofy since then, but he'll come out of it."

"Glad to hear it." I debated whether to discuss my encounter with Reich, but decided to give him the benefit of the doubt in deference to his grief. Now that he'd let off steam, he'd probably calm down. There was no reason for me to cause him to lose his job when he'd already lost his son. But just to be safe, I added, "Will you have guards out there tonight, Goose?"

"Will I have what? Where?"

I breathed in, then belted out: *"Guards! On the project!"*

"Of *course,*" he boomed back. "What kind of question is that? *What do you want?*"

"My God, Goose, I'll tell you, I'll tell you . . ."

"Oh sorry, Jenny, I was yelling at someone else. Listen, they need me, I've got to go."

"Wait a minute, Goose! Everything's okay out there?"

"Pieceacake!" I removed the phone a safe distance from my wounded ear. "If I were thirty years younger, and Jenny loved me, the world would be my oyster."

"You're full of fishy metaphors today, Goose."

"What?"

"Never mind!" I yelled back. "See you tomorrow at the groundbreaking! Good-bye!"

I don't know how he felt when he hung up, but I was exhausted. I hadn't been yelled at so much in one day since the last time I saw my sister. The call had accomplished one good deed, however: Faye was smiling, if faintly.

While she dabbed at her face with a tissue, I whirled her Rolodex again to call the eight other people who were, with Goose and me, members of the advisory committee for Liberty Harbor. We were *ex officio* in the extreme, having gravitated to the committee because of our interests in the project. As mere advisors with no legal authority, we might have been an object lesson in civic futility, but we had real influence thanks to the essential goodwill and business savvy of the private developers. They listened to our suggestions and acted on most of them. In return, we tried to be reasonable. The reward for all concerned, thus far, was an undertaking that was proceeding with remarkable ease. Ansen Reich was the first bubble on that smooth surface. I moved to pop it before it grew to explosive size.

Briefly, I told each committee member what had transpired in my office, including Reich's threat about having some power we couldn't fight, but excluding his name.

"I'm as sympathetic to his problems as the next person," was the typical response, with variations on the theme of: "But you don't have to take that kind of personal abuse, Jenny. Why, I'd have thrown the bum out on his ear."

"You and the Green Bay Packers," I replied to each of

them. "The man is seven feet tall if he's an inch. Works construction. Eats nails."

I told them what I intended to do about the situation—which was basically nothing—and asked if they had suggestions.

They didn't.

The consensus, in fact, was neatly summarized by the president of our local realtors' board.

"I think," Ted Sullivan said in his mild, pleasant way, "that you are making a sandbar out of a single grain of sand, Jenny."

This town, as you may have gathered, is unfortunately addicted to watery figures of speech. It comes from living too close, for too long, to an ocean.

"Good," I said with satisfaction to Faye when my calling was completed. "Now if red graffiti appears on the dock tomorrow, they can all share the blame with me."

"Small comfort," she said.

"Is better than no comfort at all."

Then I walked into my own office to make the additional call that would clear my conscience of Ansen Reich and his threats against the project. This time, I closed the door and dialed the number from memory.

"Sure, Jen," Police Detective Geoffrey Bushfield said when he heard my story. "I'll have the boys drive by the site more often than usual tonight. But Reich sounds like a classic bully to me, all bluff and bluster."

"Compounded by real grief, however."

"So do you want me to flash my badge at him?"

"I don't think that's necessary."

"I don't either, but I'll run him through the computer just to see what comes up on him." Then in a considerably less businesslike tone of voice, he said, "I've managed to manipulate the duty roster for this weekend, Jen, so I'll be off tomorrow night. You want to take the boat out, or not?"

"Oh yes." I sighed in a manner that is commonly known as heartfelt. "Think of it, Geof. No phones, no beepers, no walkie-talkies, no Foundation, no crimes. Just you and me and the deep blue sea."

A hearty chuckle came through the phone.

"We'll eat lobster 'til the butter runs down our chins," I continued, warming to my theme. "And we'll drink wine and ride the waves. And we'll have that talk, Geof, okay? We'll talk all night if you want to."

"I don't want to."

"What?"

"Talk all night."

"Oh." I smiled at the phone.

When I hung up that time, I felt sure I'd taken every reasonable precaution against the unreasonable rage of Ansen Reich. Now I could look forward to the groundbreaking the next day, and to our mini-vacation on Saturday night, in a relaxed frame of mind. There was nothing to worry about, nothing at all.

chapter
2

"You see, Jennifer?" said my fellow committeeman, Webster Helms, when the groundbreaking ceremony went off without a hitch the next day. The mall architect's hair was fiery under the noonday sun. "There was nothing to worry about after all, now was there?"

He all but pinched my cheek and said, "There, there."

"No, Webster," I said.

Having settled that to his satisfaction, the thin little man wheeled briskly away from me to spread his smugness, like gooey jam, elsewhere among the committee. I muttered to his straight, retreating back, "May all your freckles connect."

Beside me on the old, rotting pier, Hardy Eberhardt chuckled. "If all Web's freckles connect," the black man said, "he'll be able to qualify for minority contracts."

"Well, don't you say it, too," I said crossly. In my black linen summer suit I was sweating to an extent that is not recommended for the female who wishes to Dress for Success. "I've heard 'I told you so' from every other member of the committee, including your wife."

"Would I suggest your mysterious threatening man was but a puff of smoke?" Hardy grinned. "Why, heavens no, Jenny, I'd never be so insufferable as to intimate a thing like that."

"Oh, go jump in the bay," I suggested.

"I'd love to." He tugged at his starched shirt collar, then loosened his old school tie a quarter inch. We were killing time while the local news crews set up for group photos of the committee on the pier. Picturesque, I suppose. On three sides of us, the water of the bay winked invitingly; on the shore in front of us, Goose Shattuck's trucks and cranes were Saturday-idle. The contractor himself could be heard causing some innocent victim to go stone deaf behind us. A motley crowd had gathered ashore to watch their civic leaders baste and burn. Or maybe they were relatives: only a mother would stand out in this heat to watch her child get his picture taken. "Lord," said Hardy Eberhardt, "it's hot as a church social in Georgia on the Fourth of July."

"I guess you'd know, Reverend."

"I guess you wouldn't, Jennifer." He smiled.

I smiled back at the pastor of the First Church of the Risen Christ, this son of sharecroppers who was a graduate of the Yale School of Divinity. Tall, clean-featured and fortyish, Hardy was Port Frederick's Jesse Jackson, with a cultivated dash of Arthur Ashe. It was a potent package. I said to the magnetic minister, "One of these days I might surprise you and show up in my Sunday best for one of your famous hellfire-'n-brimstones."

"You'd cause a sensation," he said wryly. "We don't have all that many brothers and sisters whose ancestors came over on the boat from Sweden."

"I'll bet you don't." I laughed. "But you and Mary could recruit them if you set your minds to it." It was Hardy and his wife, as leaders of the local black community, who had lobbied for construction jobs and a fair share of space in the new mall for minority businesses. They'd even pushed through the name, Liberty Harbor, to symbolize the transformation of this harbor, where slave ships once were built, into a site of economic opportunity for our citizens of every

18

color. (This town not having been nicknamed "Poor Fred" for nothing!) "I do believe the two of you could sell sand to Sudan, so it should be no problem for you to convince a few Swedes that we originally descended from African tribes."

Hardy's belly laugh was deep and infectious enough to attract attention. A photographer from the Port Frederick *Times* turned to snap us.

"That'll make a nice black-and-white glossy," I said. But Hardy didn't laugh this time.

"Now I've done it." His eyes narrowed. "Get your picture in the paper with me and you'll get real threats, for sure."

"You're kidding." I peered more closely into those intense brown eyes. "You're not kidding?"

"People!" A few feet away, Mary Eberhardt clapped her hands twice. "They're ready for us! Let's get this show on the road!"

"My wife," Hardy said, a fond smile playing on his lips, "always wanted to be a cheerleader. I tell her that being a minister's wife amounts to the same thing, but she is not convinced."

We ambled toward centerstage on the pier where the eight other members of our committee were gathering, prodded by gentle shoves from Mary Eberhardt. In her soft pink summer dress and her straw hat with pink ribbons, she looked less like a cheerleader than like Mary of nursery-rhyme fame, herding her lazy sheep. "Here, Webster," she commanded. "Not there, Jenny, back here beside Goose."

"Yes, Mary," I said.

"Yes, dear." Her husband smiled.

In friendly confusion, the ten of us assumed stiff, false poses under the noonday sun, our backs to the bay, our faces toward the spectators. Behind them, low hills rose steeply to the highway from which we heard a barely perceptible hum. I watched idly as a green pickup truck turned from the highway onto the cul-de-sac that was a lover's leap in my day. On this day, a couple of cars were already parked there, although probably for curiosity's sake, not for romance. Through years of neglect, the waterfront had become too derelict, too smelly for romance. As I stood on the pier, gazing up into the sun, I mused dreamily that with the renovation, the old lover's leap might once again become the spot where whole new generations of horny teenagers would come of age in the back seat of Chevys. Or was it Toyotas now?

"You'd think I'd outgrow these damn things," muttered the man on my left, snapping me out of my reverie. It was seventy-eight-year-old Jack Fenton, chairman of the board of First City Bank, which was a major lender to the project. He was also a trustee of the Foundation, which made him one of my bosses. This day, his usual good humor seemed to be melting; even his seersucker suit drooped. He added to no one in particular, "I'm certainly old enough to know better."

Nobody answered him. We were too hot.

As the tallest woman, I stood in back between Jack Fenton and Goose Shattuck, with the Reverend Hardy Eberhardt on the far side of Goose and Ted Sullivan, the realtor, on the other side of Jack. Up front, there was Mary Eberhardt; the little redheaded architect, Webster Helms; our mayor, Barbara Schneider; and Pierre and Brigitte Latour, aka Pete and Betty Tower to us locals. The Towers— or Latours—were building a French café beside the old lobster pound which lay between the hills and the bay. Our mayor stood where she always stands, on the far right side of things, directly opposite Hardy Eberhardt. When I saw their positions, I smiled to myself at the unconscious symbolism of it all.

"Where's your maniac, Jenny?" the mayor inquired sweetly, as we all put on our civic smiles. Some of the others broke into laughter at Jenny's paranoia. Adding insult to injury, the mayor looked cool and immaculate in polished cotton. She said, "Maybe you'll be good enough to point him out to us, so we can duck his can of spray paint?"

"May all your children be Democrats, Barbara," I replied.

"Bite your tongue!" the mayor said.

Beside me, Goose boomed, "What maniac?"

I pretended not to hear him, an act which I will admit

requires some pretty heavy pretending. I still had no desire to besmirch Reich's name with his employer, especially since Reich had come up clean in the police computer, the only record he had being a distinguished military one. So I let my attention be snagged by the sun as it glinted off the windshield of the green pickup truck on top of the hill. Instead of stopping at lover's leap to admire the view, it was coming on straight, giving a momentary impression that it would dive off the top of the hill into the filthy old lobster pound directly below. It didn't, of course; it merely turned onto the temporary dirt road that served as a shortcut to the highway for the construction crews.

"Smile!" a photographer commanded, fatuously.

"Move closer together!" yelled another one.

"No!" we yelled back, the committee being for once in unison.

Cameras began to whir and click.

In the unrelenting heat, I began to feel queasy. Thinking it might refresh me, I glanced down at the water through the cracks in the floor of the old pier. Immediately, I was mesmerized by the waves that licked the wood beneath our feet. So lost in a stupor was I that I barely heard Mary Eberhardt's small, sharp voice.

"Isn't he coming kind of fast?" was all she said.

I looked up, in that odd moment of frozen silence, to see the green pickup hurtling at high speed down the steep construction path, straight toward the very pier on which we stood.

"Oh, my God," the mayor exclaimed.

"Run!" Ted Sullivan yelled. Then, *"Run! Run!"*

"Where?" we screamed.

Indeed, there was nowhere to run, our sole route of escape being right in the path of the truck. Already, the spectators on the shore had scattered, screaming, as the truck roared through them. Now they stared in horrified fascination at their civic leaders as we stood like bowling pins at the end of a long, rickety, wooden alley.

"Oh!" Betty Tower screamed.

The truck was so close by now that we could hear its tires

strike rocks and sand. Then they hit the wood on the edge of the pier with a terrible splintering sound. I stared directly into the cab of the truck and saw clearly a giant of a man. His eyes were wide, his mouth an open scream, his hands fastened fanatically on the wheel.

"Jump!" I screamed, in concert with several others. *"Jump! Now!"*

I dived headfirst off the left side of the pier, while camera crews and committee members leaped like a tossed salad into the water on either side.

When I surfaced, I was gagging on oily, lukewarm seawater. In my linen suit, I treaded water with my committee members and the members of the press. We could only watch helplessly, horror-stricken, as Ansen Reich sped off the end of the pier into seventy-five feet of saltwater.

chapter
3

I saw Detective Geoffrey Bushfield a little earlier than planned that Saturday. He arrived at the harbor, accompanied by a screaming fleet of police cars and firetrucks. Soon, an ambulance was parked on the construction path down which Reich had rushed to his death. For all the good the ambulance could do, they might as well have sent a taxi.

Soon, too, I was arguing with the detective, who was beginning to look as if he'd like to send me home in a taxi.

"But Geof," I entreated, "you once told me that you catch more criminals by the application of common sense than by the application of criminology. So don't give me this baloney about regulations."

He observed me dryly, in more ways than one, from a safe distance.

As I squeezed a hank of my hair, like a towel, with both hands, I said, "I want to go with you when you tell Reich's wife. Your common sense ought to tell you that's a good idea."

He sighed, so that his broad shoulders moved within the confines of his well-tailored jacket.

"I seem to be testifying against myself," he said irritably. "Look, if I'm going to break the rules, at least give me some justification for the benefit of my so-called superiors." I knew I'd won the argument then, which was no surprise since the man had been breaking one rule or another most of his life.

"I'm the one who knows why he did it," I pointed out in a reasonable tone of voice. I picked up my shoes from the ground and let the remaining water trickle out the heels. "And I was an eyewitness to his death, so I can give his wife a firsthand account if she wants it."

"You were not an eyewitness to his death," Geof said, in the same tone of voice in which people say, "Will you please not crack your knuckles?" "You were an eyewitness only to his coming down the pier toward you. Nobody but the fishies actually saw him die."

"Fishies?"

He started to laugh first, followed quickly by me.

"Geof," I said then, in a softer tone, "I really want to go. It's important to me. I feel responsible for . . ."

"Talk about baloney," he interrupted, and shook a long finger at me. "I know you, Jennifer Cain, and if there's a load of guilt to haul, you'll pack it up and carry it away on your shoulders, even if it doesn't belong to you . . ."

"Geof!"

His young partner, Ailey Mason, trotted up. He was panting in the heat.

"Geof," he said, "the divers have found the truck."

"How soon before they pull him out?"

"Soon."

"All right. I'll wait to get official confirmation that he's dead before I leave for his house."

"Before we leave," I corrected him sweetly.

Mason glanced at Geof, then at me. His eyes traveled from my hair, which lay in strings on my shoulders, down my sodden suit to which unnamable green things clung, to my stockinged feet.

"What did you use for bait, Geof?" he said.

"Mason!" Geof growled, so that the young policeman took off running again, back toward the pier to watch the salvage operation.

"Sorry, Jenny."

But I was smiling, for once having found Ailey Mason amusing. I did, after all, look like something Jacques Cousteau had not only dredged up, but would most likely throw back. I was grateful to Mason for leavening this sad afternoon with a moment of malicious wit. But when I thought once again of the widow who waited, unknowing, my smile disappeared.

"So when do we leave, Geof?" I said quietly.

Behind his sunglasses, his brown eyes looked at something grim over my head. Suddenly, I heard shouts and splashing.

"Now," the detective said.

The house was a basic ranch, a style that is more indigenous to the Midwest than to our eastern coast, and out of place among the Cape Cods that lined the block. Because it stretched out longer on its lot than they did, it looked larger than its peers. As had its owner. It had an air of good repair and new paint, as if Reich had applied his construction skills at home. The house was yellow, of a shade too far-gone into mustard for beauty; the window-frames, shutters and front door were brown. Not, I suspected, a popular house with the neighbors.

"Ready?" Geof removed the key from the ignition of the police sedan. He looked at me as I tried to repair myself in the broken shard of mirror on the back side of the sun visor. I looked like a drowned rat that had dried, then applied lipstick and mascara. He said, "Are you sure you want to do this, Jenny? There's no guarantee that she will like you any better than he did, you know. If you think he was nuts, you may find she sets a whole new standard of hysteria."

"That happens?"

He shot me a look that said he knew I was stalling.

"Of course it happens," he said patiently, "especially if

they didn't get along. Show me a wife who hates her husband when he's alive, and I'll show you wailing and gnashing of teeth when he dies."

"Maybe she loved him."

"Then it will be worse, in a different way. Those are the ones I hate, the ones where you're bringing real pain, and they try to be so brave so you won't feel bad about it. Jesus!" He stuffed the keys in his coat pocket. "And don't forget it was her son, too."

"I haven't forgotten, Geof."

"Yeah." He shook his head, then looked out the window away from me. "What an incredibly stupid thing for me to say. I'm sorry, Jen. I don't know what the hell's wrong with me today, I'm as irritable as a crab with an itch."

"It's the weather," I said charitably. "Besides, just so long as one of us is always right."

Still looking out the window, he grinned.

I shot a last glance at the mirror, gave it up as a lost cause, and flipped up the visor. By one of those mutual silent accords into which we often fell, Geof and I opened our respective doors and got out of the car, meeting on the curb in front of the Reich house. Side by side, we walked reluctantly up the cement steps to the ugly brown door. Most of the neighbors' steps and walks were handlaid stones.

"You introduce me, all right?" I said. I was nervous. "I'll chime in with my story whenever it seems appropriate."

"Right." He glanced down at me. "You have, I've noticed, a highly developed sense of the appropriate moment."

"Good breeding," I said shakily, "shows."

He spanned the back of my neck with his hard right hand and squeezed, briefly, gently. With his other hand, he rang the doorbell.

"Yes?" said the woman who answered the door. She was Hera to Reich's Zeus, a thick, handsome pole of a woman who could obviously hurl thunderbolts of her own. "Yes, what is it?"

"Are you Annie Reich, Mrs. Ansen Reich?" Geof asked. As a rookie, he'd told the wrong woman her husband was dead. It was the man's aunt, or something, whose real husband was in intensive care somewhere with a coronary. By the time things got straight, the aunt had fainted, the real wife had threatened to murder Geof, and his captain had wondered loudly and profanely if G. Bushfield was really cut out for police work. Since then, he always checked to see if the person to whom he was giving the news was the person to whom the news belonged.

This woman nodded affirmatively.

Annie and Ansen, I thought then; names for a cute little couple with button noses, not these Germanic giants.

"Mrs. Reich," Geof was saying sadly, "I'm Geof Bushfield with the Port Frederick police department." He opened his wallet to prove it. She glanced at his ID. When she looked up again, the expression in her navy blue eyes had changed. "And this is, uh, Ms. Jennifer Cain." Perhaps he thought it best to let her think, for the moment, that I was also a cop. "Could we come in, Mrs. Reich?"

"No," she said, but not unpleasantly. Just firm. And who among us could have moved this woman if she chose not to budge? "Tell me."

"It's your husband." Geof looked her full in the face. "He drove his truck into a crowd of spectators at the ground-breaking ceremonies at Liberty Harbor this afternoon. No one else was hurt, but your husband's truck went off the end of the pier into the bay. He's dead. I'm sorry."

She looked at me for the first time, as if I might fill in some sort of blank.

"He was distraught over the death of your son, Mrs. Reich," I said, trying not to stammer. "That's why it happened, that's why he did it. He was crazy with grief."

The steady, navy blue eyes traveled back to Geof, then returned to me. "Ansen, crazy with grief?" said the Widow Reich. "Don't make me laugh."

chapter
4

She let us in then, closing the door behind us as decisively as I suspected she did everything else in life. Her home smelled strongly of Clorox. The rooms held normal amounts of furniture, but they were pieces built for a race of giants, so the house had an overstuffed air about it. I began to get that panicky flutter at the bottom of my stomach that comes with claustrophobia.

"In there." She pointed us into a family room. I expected lightning to flash from her extended finger. My Lord, the woman was majestic. "I'll bring iced tea."

"I guess we're having iced tea," Geof whispered down the back of my neck. "I wonder if I'm having mine with sugar or without."

"She'll let you know," I whispered back.

The family room was misnamed. There was nothing there to indicate a family had ever inhabited it—no pictures of the father, the mother, the son or any other person. No games, no clutter, no stereo, radio or television. Just more of that big furniture, and a single shelf that ran around all four walls of the room. The shelf had evidently been constructed for the sole purpose of displaying an impressive collection of beer steins, the sculptured kind with the silver lids that crack down on the bridge of your nose if you drink too exuberantly. Perhaps the Reichs had drunk beer out of different mugs each evening, sitting in the huge armchairs, facing each other, talking about their days. My mind veered off onto one of its fantasies: what a splendid place to have a drunken brawl, I thought . . . so many beer mugs to hurl, so few things to break.

I sank into one of the armchairs, feeling like Goldilocks having found Papa Bear's chair.

Geof perched on the front edge of the couch as if he were afraid he'd fall in and never be seen again. He threw me the same look that Hansel must have thrown Gretel about the time they got an idea of what the big oven was for.

"If this is hysterical," I said to him, "I would like to see her when she's calm."

"Maybe goddesses don't grieve." It seemed his thoughts were running along the same mythological track as mine.

"Are you kidding? Don't you remember what Demeter did when Pluto kidnapped Persephone?"

"No." He grinned at me. "Would we have a record of it at the station?"

I reached over to give his wrist an affectionate pat just as she walked back into the family room. Those clear navy eyes watched my hand snake back into my lap. I felt as guilty as a child whose mother has caught it playing doctor. Don't be absurd, I told myself, she's only a bereaved woman, not an avenging Valkyrie. Nevertheless, I crossed my legs at the ankles, sat up straighter and clasped my hands primly in my lap. Out of the corner of my eye, I saw Geof surreptitiously rub the toe of his right shoe against the back of his left trouser leg. I suppressed a smile.

She extended a wooden tray to me.

"Thank you," I said.

Geof took a sip of the iced tea she handed to him. "Um," he murmured, not looking at me. "Nice and sweet."

She sat in an armchair which was a twin to mine. It fit her just fine. "Now tell me from the beginning," she said. "What has the damn fool done now?"

I began to wonder if the fact that he was dead had sunk in upon her. But she could hardly miss the point as Geof painstakingly explained what happened at the pier. Annie Reich listened without interrupting, her hands lying still on the armrests, her mouth closed, her eyes wide and expressionless. I might have suspected she was asleep with her eyes open if it hadn't been for the deepening crease between her eyes. She looked a bit put out.

"Mrs. Reich," Geof said, as he stumbled to a close without any comment from her. "Ms. Cain is the executive director of the Port Frederick Civic Foundation. She was present when your husband died, and she can tell you more about why we think he did it."

The large handsome head swiveled my way. The unblinking eyes fastened on me.

"Your husband came to my office yesterday, Mrs. Reich," I said. "He was angry at me and at our Foundation, because he thought we could have prevented your son's death."

"Could you have?"

"No."

"Why did he think that?"

"You don't know?" I shook my head to clear it. "No, of course you don't, or you wouldn't ask." For the first time, a glimmer of humor crossed her broad face. Taking heart, I continued. "As I understand it, your son tried to call the suicide center for several hours before he finally, uh . . . He wasn't able to get help from there, however, because they hadn't paid their phone bill in three months and their service had been shut off that day." That sounded so unbelievable even to me that I felt compelled to explain. "I know that sounds unconscionable, and perhaps it was, but the thing about volunteer organizations is that they are usually broke, and sometimes they run more on good intentions than good management. I'm afraid that was the case with the center . . . the left hand thought the right hand had paid the bill, but in effect, neither hand had written the check." I paused, aware that I might have gotten a little carried away with my own figures of speech. Geof's face wore a familiar bemused expression. I said quickly, "The Foundation is not permitted to fund organizations outside of town, so ordinarily the center wouldn't come to us for help. My secretary works as a volunteer there, however; when she learned of their predicament, she called me to see if I could pay their bill out of my personal funds. I did that, but the service was not restored in time to help your son."

I took a breath.

She waited.

"S-so," I stammered, "so . . . your husband got the idea it was all our fault, and nothing I could say seemed to convince him otherwise. When he came to our office, he made threats against Liberty Harbor, out of some mis- guided idea of revenge. I guess he knew how important that project is to the Foundation and to this town, and he thought that's where he could hurt us the most. And that's why he did what he did . . . out of grief, I suppose."

One large hand moved on the armrest of her chair, as if in mild protest.

"Phillip was not his son," she said.

Geof and I looked at each other in surprise.

"He was my boy from my first marriage. He and my . . ."—she smiled—"late husband could not stand each other. You think Ansen killed himself out of grief over Philly? Hah!" Her smile broadened, as if what she'd said were actually funny. I felt a shiver cross my shoulders. "It was an accident, that's all, one of Ansen's crazy jokes. He just wanted to scare you people for some crazy reason of his own." She chuckled. "But he scared himself, I'll bet . . . scared himself to death!"

We stared at her. Was this the limit of the woman's emotional range? Was this macabre humor all she felt, this woman who'd lost a son and a husband in the span of a few short days? Suddenly, I was aware of exactly what had been bothering me since we'd entered her house. Where were the family and friends who should be here to comfort her in her bereavement for her son? There should have been the quiet talk and laughter of people who cared, and the comforting smell of food that kindly neighbors had brought over. Instead, her house was empty, silent, eerie. I felt an unkind and intense desire to prick that smooth white hide to see if warm blood—or tears—ran within her.

"It was an accident," she said with finality. "Would you like more iced tea?"

"Iced tea?" Again, I shook my head to clear it of the heaviness this woman and her overstuffed house induced. "No, thank you. Is there anything else you'd like to know, Mrs. Reich?"

She looked puzzled, as if that were an odd question. But she turned to Geof. "You'll tell me where you take his body, I suppose."

"You tell us, Mrs. Reich."

Again, that puzzled expression. "I don't know. Is there a funeral home that's close by? That won't charge me an arm and a leg?" Her allusion brought to my mind an image of her husband's corpse, and was oddly distasteful; more than that, repellent.

I said through gritted teeth, "The Harbor Lights Funeral Home is dependable."

"All right," she said agreeably. "Why don't you send him there?" For all the emotion she showed, she might have been having a pizza sent to a friend's house. But then she seemed to sense for once that something more in the way of conversation might be appropriate. "We only moved here for this job, you see, from Springfield."

Well, that meant they had only been in town for a few weeks, which explained several things, including why I had not previously seen or heard of them.

We seized the appropriate moment to say good-bye.

In the car, Geof turned the key in the ignition, then suddenly smiled.

"What?" I said.

"I suppose there's one thing that can be said in Reich's favor."

"What's that?"

"I'll bet he didn't beat his wife."

I was still laughing when we pulled away from the curb. I happened to glance back at the Reich house, in time to see a broad face disappear from the living room window. A curtain fell back into place.

"Damn." The laughter died in my throat. She'd probably seen me laughing; I felt insensitive and tactless.

"What, hon?"

"I need a vacation."

"Well, aren't you the lucky one? We just happen to have an opening on our Saturday night cruise which leaves the fabulous Port Frederick Marina this very evening."

"Will I have to share a stateroom?" I leaned my head wearily against the headrest.

"What do you expect with such late reservations?" We turned a corner, and Geof looked over at me. His expression had turned serious, probing. "Do you have any reservations about this weekend, Jenny?"

"No." I closed my eyes.

"In that case," he said more lightly, "you may have to share a bed, as well."

I replied to that provocative suggestion by falling asleep.

chapter
5

We pulled away from the marina—not to be confused with Liberty Harbor which inhabited another bay—after the sun was well on its way to California for the night. We were aboard the *Amy Denise,* a forty-two-foot trawler that Ted Sullivan had lent us for the weekend. It wasn't that Geof or I couldn't afford boats of our own; we both came from families whose trust funds provided sufficient income to purchase fleets for small South American countries. No, we had the boat for the night because, as Geof said when he brought home Ted's invitation, "Over the years, I'll bet Ted and I have exchanged just about everything with a motor or an engine. Cars, lawn mowers, motorcycles. Last winter, I lent him my snow blower, so now we get his boat."

"Nice going," I'd replied, "do you think he's got a week on a schooner he'd trade for a day with my Cuisinart?"

Actually, I thought we were doing Ted the favor by taking his boat out for a good run to warm the winter out of her. As the whole town knew, the realtor had not been able to bring himself to use the *Amy Denise* since his wife for whom it was named had left him, as they say, for another. Local wisdom had it that the boat represented especially painful memories because Amy Denise had given it to Ted as an anniversary present.

As I lounged on a bench beside Geof who had the helm on the bridge, I raised my vodka-and-tonic in a silent toast to our absent host.

"It's nice of Ted to let other people get some pleasure from his boat," I said aloud, "even if he can't. Or won't. I wonder why he doesn't just sell her, memories and all."

"Maybe he hopes Amy will come back aboard one day." Geof shook his head; his thick shock of brown hair ruffled in the wind. "He's more patient than I am." He glanced back over his bare shoulder at me. "Maybe we should make him an offer, eh, mate?"

Mate.

I searched his face to see if he'd intended the double meaning, but the handsome features only looked tired, neutral. When I only smiled in reply, he turned back to the open sea.

We were mates of a sort, and had been ever since tragedy had brought us together a half year ago. He was twice married and divorced; at thirty, I was single by choice and circumstance. The attraction between us had been immediate and compelling, and we had not hesitated to live together in that never-never land, for which there is no name, between dating and marriage. We were the odd couple: the former bad boy from a good family and the girl from a good family that had gone bad. My background was well known around town. His was not, partly because his family had moved away the year he'd graduated from high school, four years before me—and partly because when he returned to his hometown to fulfill his teenage dream of being a cop, he had not encouraged people to connect the tall, serious policeman with the wild kid of fifteen years earlier. Most of his former juvenile-delinquent buddies had long since drifted away to lesser fates; only a few old pals, like Ted Sullivan, were still around to connect the cop with Bushware, Inc., plumbing and hardware supply companies in the Northeast. So he remained fairly anonymous. Until he began dating me. Now we were a delicious source of local gossip.

"Geof?"

Again, a turn of his head. And this time, a quick, warm smile. "Jenny?"

I leaned back against the rail that was wet with cool ocean spray. "Nothing," I said.

Together, we stared into the silent darkness ahead. Behind and to the sides of us, lights flickered cozily on the shore. It was like our relationship, I thought: the safety of conventionality lay all around us, winking and beckoning like an old friend of the family with whom we might feel comfortable—while ahead lay territory that held more risk by virtue of being less well charted. Though not noticeably successful at it, Geof liked being married. But I had no family model upon which to base any hope for marital bliss. And while I certainly had faith in him as a person, I wasn't sure I'd bet the rent on his prospects as a husband. Still, we could not drift forever, like teenagers, in that foggy, foolish world of not-quite-committed. It was fish-or-cut-bait time, and I was scared. I didn't want to lose him.

And yet . . .

A stomach rumbled.

"Was that yours or mine?" he asked.

"Yours." I laughed. Leave it to the human body to pull the mind back down to ground level. Or sea level, as it were. I said, "I'll go below and start dinner. I can take a hint."

He had us securely anchored in a quiet cove by the time I had dinner on the table across from the galley. It had not taken much searching to find Amy Sullivan's cache of plastic plates, rust-proof pans, washable placemats and paper napkins. They were immaculate and neatly stacked in the cupboards, as if Amy had just left for home, instead of having left home entirely. It had been a standing joke among Ted's friends that he and Amy Denise would retire on this boat in another few years, thus living out Ted's teenage dream of retiring when he reached Jack Benny's age. But while Ted dreamed of the South Seas, Amy had stood in this galley, peeling carrots and dreaming of her lover. Maybe she was in Tahiti with him now; that would be an ironic and unkind twist of fate. But I smiled, thinking it wasn't likely. Above her sink a small wooden plaque read, "A boat is a hole in the water into which you pour money." On the refrigerator, a magnet said, "Frankly, I'd rather drive." And, stitched onto a teatowel was the motto, "If the Good Lord had meant man to swim, He'd have furnished fins." Wherever Amy was, it wasn't on a boat! I felt sorry for Ted, and I didn't admire the cowardly way she left him; but part of me was cheered by the sheer audacity of her departure. If sweet, neat little Amy Denise, that archetypal housewife, could up and leave with a lover, there was hope for other conventional, predictable people. Feeling optimistic, I hollered up the ladder for Geof to come to supper.

Twenty gluttonous minutes later, he said, "There's butter on your chin. No, don't wipe it off. It's sexy." He leered. "I'll lick it off later."

"Actually, it's margarine."

"Oh." He handed me a napkin. "Not so sexy."

We were having lobsters, as planned, as well as steamed clams, although steamers always reminded me of my father. And that always left a bitter aftertaste that had nothing to do with clams. It took me a year to be able to eat clams again after my father, in his amiable way, ran three generations of Cain Clams into bankruptcy during my junior year in college. Even now, it was hard to choke them down over the memory of the employees he put out of work, and the memory of my mother and younger sister whose familial guilt nearly destroyed them. I was made of tougher—or less sensitive—stuff, I guess. The shame merely drove me into work of a charitable nature. And away from clams.

"Jenny," Geof said suddenly, "I want to ask you something."

He looked unusually serious, uncharacteristically hesitant.

No! I thought in a panic. Please don't ask me!

"All right," I said.

"Which Reich did you believe?"

I breathed again.

"He was very convincing, Geof."

"So you think he did kill himself out of grief?"

I dunked a hunk of Italian bread in the drawn butter. Er, margarine. "Well," I conceded, "he might not have intended to kill himself. But what was his reason for attacking the rest of us, if not grief or revenge or guilt?"

"But why would she lie about him?" he insisted. He was pushing me into the position of devil's advocate, as he did with Ailey Mason when they were on a case.

"Maybe she didn't lie," I extemporized. "Maybe she only perceived him differently, through the bitter lens of their marriage."

He smiled, but whether at my conclusion or my imagery, I couldn't tell.

"Anyway," I said impatiently, "what difference does it make, Geof? The man is dead, whether by accident or by his own design. Nobody else was hurt. It's over and done. Right?"

"I don't like the unfinished feel of it," he said slowly. "And I especially don't like contradictory explanations of violent death."

"Violent?" I scoffed. "All things considered, he really went fairly quietly into the bay, Geof. I mean, nobody pushed him."

"Neither did he die in his sleep, Jenny."

"The problem with you," I said then, "is that you're a detective with nothing to detect."

He laughed, then ate the last bites of lobster. A few minutes later he said, "Well, we're having the truck raised, so maybe we'll find out if it was an accident or if it was suicide. If it looks as if the brakes failed, for instance, we'll know it was accidental death, and that his wife was right, after all."

A thought occurred to me.

"It could be important for her to be right," I said.

"Yes, if there's insurance."

He refilled my glass of wine. We sipped in compatible silence. When I finally broke it, any thoughts of Ansen Reich were far away.

"I'll wash," I said, "if you'll dry."

"You'd think we were married," he said blandly.

I suddenly discovered a lobster claw that demanded my full and immediate attention.

Later, in the aft stateroom, we shed our swimsuits and looked ironically at each other in the romantic light of the moon that shone down through the open hatch above the bed.

"The mind is willing," Geof said with a crooked smile that should have been devastatingly irresistible, "but the body is failing."

"I know," I agreed, wearily.

We stood so close together in the cramped space that it was impossible not to hug, so we did at least take advantage of that opportunity. It was, however, more of a mutual propping up than an embrace.

I sighed against his chest. "Tonight I feel the hot breath of middle age upon my neck."

"That's not middle age," he said, "that's me."

We snickered, I into the hair on his chest, he into the hair on top of my head. Our subsequent good-night kiss was more fond than fervid. We collapsed onto opposite sides of the double bed and pulled a single sheet over us.

His voice roused me from near-sleep.

"Jenny, do you remember at dinner tonight when I told you I wanted to ask you something?"

"Sure, hon."

"And you know the talk we were going to have this weekend?"

"Yes." I hoped he didn't want to have it now. Our plans had not included this extraordinary day which had drained and exhausted both of us.

"We probably don't need to have that talk," he said. "The

look on your face at that moment told me everything I need to know."

"Geof . . ."

"Go to sleep, darling Jenny."

"I do love you."

But he had turned to the wall. In the dark, his breathing was slow and even.

chapter
6

I, however, could not sleep.

The moon beamed too brightly through the hatch. Geof breathed too raggedly. The boat rocked instead of rolled. My eyes remained wide open like windows propped up on an otherwise sagging house. I was so tired my head hurt. Still, I couldn't sleep. Instead, my mind insisted on reliving the terrifying moment of my plunge into Liberty Harbor Bay. From there, the synapses snapped back into a family room where giants quaffed iced tea from monstrous mugs. Then my thoughts jumped back to the man in bed beside me and feelings of frustration swept remembered fear out to sea.

Again, I leaped into the bay.

Back to Annie Reich's house.

To wed, or merely to bed?

Quietly, I removed the sheet from my body. I swung my bare legs over the side of the bed. Rising slowly from the mattress to avoid squeaks, I looked back at Geof to be sure I did not wake him. At least one of us should get some rest on this long hot night.

Still nude, I climbed the steps to the main deck. In the galley, I mixed myself a weak bourbon-and-water, no ice, thinking it might have the soporific effect of a glass of warm milk.

With the nightcap to keep me company, I climbed the ladder to the bridge. I lay on the deck, rested the glass on my bare stomach and stared up at the stars in the Massachusetts sky, intending to meditate myself to sleep. I tried to manage a sip from the drink. It spilled down my bare chest.

"Damn."

I sat up precipitously.

So much for meditation under the starry night sky. Anyway, I felt itchy, as if I could run for miles.

"All right," I finally said to myself, "why not?"

The night was clear, I knew this coastline well by day or night, so why not *move?* Within minutes, I had the anchor raised and the engines going.

The act of having to concentrate on running the boat relaxed me as nothing else had been able to do. By the time I puttered around the third cove into Liberty Harbor Bay, I was loose-limbed and vaguely content with the universe once more.

I rang the ship's bell.

"Two o'clock and all's swell!" I sang out into the night, and laughed. The boat and I were buoyant. She responded easily to my direction, though she rolled a bit as trawlers will. I braced my feet wide and grasped the wheel firmly to hold her steady. I was still naked as a fish.

I throttled back still more, with the idea of anchoring just off-shore, out of traffic. On land, straight ahead, the renovation project was outlined against the sky like a stick city, all steel beams and tall cranes.

It was beautiful, this natural harbor that was spread out before me; it was man who'd ruined it, one man in particular. I remembered old Lobster McGee, gone now two lobstering seasons after a drowning at sea, but only from the surly distance he had imposed between himself and the rest of the world. There'd been a nephew once who went lobstering with his cantankerous uncle, but the kid died in Vietnam. After that, Lobster let his stretch of bayfront property go to hell so that anyone with a sense of smell avoided his harbor, probably just as he wanted. We'd see him now and then at The Buoy, our local pub, standing apart from the other fishermen, drinking his draw in malevolent solitude. During the lobstering seasons, he'd looked healthy and strong as if the very work enlarged him; but in the off seasons, he'd seemed to shrink, his barrel chest caving in, his girth melting as if, like his lobsters, he'd shed his shell. It made him no more friendly, however; if anything, less so.

He was a character all right, the sort who gets whitewashed into legends. The Coast Guard had towed his boat home when they found it floating without him. Now it bobbed at one of the new docks, waiting to be turned into a display for posterity. Lobster would definitely have puked.

From my vantage point on the *Amy Denise,* I surveyed the property his heirs had sold to the developers. To starboard was his three-story house which would be transformed into a cultural center. Rumor had it that when Lobster's bedroom was opened, all the first visitors found there were dirty clothes, massive walnut furniture, a week's worth of newspapers, a telescope turned appropriately to the sea and three hundred and forty-two paperbags from McDonald's. Soon that remarkable bedroom would be a pictorial gallery of the history of fishing in the Northeast. It had been suggested that we bronze one of the moldy french fries and display it with a commemorative plaque, but our committee vetoed the idea.

To port of the old house, and directly below lover's leap, was the old man's lobster pound which was actually just a small, saltwater pond which the old man had probably not drained and cleaned for all the forty years he'd lived there. Now it belonged to Pete and Betty Tower, who would use it to store fresh lobsters for their café. At the moment, however, they were continuing Lobster's habit of keeping shedders—lobsters which are growing new shells—in it.

Shedders have to be fed a regular diet of fish parts, thus adding to the unappetizing stew—and the stench on hot days.

Past the pound and the site of the French café, a ship-building school was going up, and a three-story mall that was the heart of the project. In Webster Helms' architectural renderings, the mall was a charming, old-fashioned marketplace that was alive with colors, sounds and fabulous aromas. We on the committee hoped the primary color would be green, with an occasional flash of American Express gold and platinum, and the principal sound would be, "Yes, I'll take it."

I nosed the *Amy Denise* into the breeze that was wafting down from lover's leap.

A shooting star fell. It was achingly lovely, a glow of reddish white against a navy sky, arching over the construction site so it seemed to fall into the sea. I imagined a sizzle, and laughed at my fantasy.

Quickly, another star descended, then another. I realized I was going to be privileged to witness a meteor shower. A strong gust of wind down from the hills brought the falling stars even closer, so they flared like fire coming toward me.

"Oh my God."

The "shooting star" landed with a crackle on a canvas deck chair. The evening paper on the seat of the chair burst into flames.

"Oh my God!"

There was nothing on hand to smother the fire; we'd taken our towels below. Flaming bits of paper were floating in the wind, being carried dangerously about the deck. In a very few moments, I would have a monstrous problem on my very bare hands.

"Geof!" I screamed, then more usefully, *"Fire!"*

I ran to the controls on the bridge, looking for a fire extinguisher, but when I found it I had to stop to read the directions. The absurdity of it all nearly undid me. It was difficult to read in the darkness that was fitfully lit by fire. When I finally figured things out, I aimed the extinguisher at the bonfire on the seat of the deck chair.

Nothing happened.

Then with a whoosh, foam gushed out of the extinguisher. After dousing the chair, I turned the foam onto the other spreading circles of fire. In mercifully quick order, my days as a firefighter were successfully ended.

I dropped the empty extinguisher to the deck.

Geof plunged, late and bare-assed, over the top of the ladder. "What the hell happened?" He stared at me, then all around me at the ashtray the bridge had become.

I took a deep breath, then let it out very slowly. "Where's your Dalmation?" I said shakily.

But his gaze had been diverted to the shore.

I turned to stare, too.

At the project, the architect's shack was blazing like an autumn bonfire. And what was left of the rickety old pier that Reich had plunged off was ablaze as well.

I looked up at lover's leap with a whole new perspective on the wonders of nature. The "meteor shower" had stopped. Somebody had taken his rag-tipped, kerosene-soaked arrows and gone home.

"Are you all right?" Geof said.

"Yes, no thanks to Robin Flaming Hood."

Lights—electric ones—began to glow at the project.

"Discretion being the better part of valor," Geof said, "we'd better get dressed. You sure you're all right?" When I nodded, he said, "Can you get to a phone on shore?"

"I suppose the private guards will let me use the phone in Goose Shattuck's office. Why?"

"I want you to call Shattuck and get him down here."

Half an hour later, I did call him.

"Goose." I was perched on a corner of his desk. "This is Jennifer Cain. I'm sorry to disturb you at this hour, but there's been some trouble at the harbor. Somebody has set fire to Webster Helms' shack, and there's some other minor fire damage as well. Can you get dressed and come on down here?"

He uttered a remarkably imaginative curse. Then he said, sounding wide awake for that hour, "I'm already dressed, but I can't get there from here, Miss Jenny. Some son-of-a-bitch has slashed all the tires on all the vehicles I own: my pickup; the Caddy; my wife's car; my daughter's minibike, for Christ's sake. What the hell's going on, Jenny? Huh?" His voice rose to a roar that would wake his neighbors. "My foreman's dead. Somebody immobilizes me. Now you tell me they've tried to burn me out. What the hell is going on, Jenny!"

I couldn't tell him.

chapter
7

Through the night and early morning, the cops sifted through the ashes for metal tips and bits of arrows. They searched lover's leap for the evidence they didn't really hope to find: footprints, tire prints, dropped belongings. The archer had been neat and careful, sweeping his tracks with a broom of pine needles.

"Nothing," Geof paused long enough to say about 4 A.M. And then a couple of hours later, "Nothing."

"At least he didn't do real damage," I said. "The only total loss is the architect's shack. And Goose can build him another one in the time it takes to nail together a few boards. It'll probably take him longer to replace his tires." I peered into the face of the weary policeman who stood before me. "What does all this mean, Geof?"

"Beats the hell out of me." He shrugged.

By nine that morning, we were at police headquarters. Nobody seemed to object to the presence of the tall blonde in the red shorts and white T-shirt who was following Detective Bushfield around the station, so I remained with him.

After bad coffee and worse doughnuts, we dropped off Geof's collection of ashes and burnt arrowheads at the evidence room, then walked two flights down to the police garage.

My rubber thongs flapped noisily against my heels.

Geof was even more out of uniform, even for a plain-clothes cop. He wore the only clothes he'd taken aboard the *Amy Denise:* yellow boxer swim trunks, a Mexican shirt that hung loose to his hip bones and ratty old deck shoes. He would have looked more at home doing undercover drug work in Cancún.

When we walked into the garage, a black face appeared from under Ansen Reich's pickup truck which was up on a hydraulic lift.

"Detective," said the young mechanic, and flashed a shy smile at me. He dived back under the truck as if further conversation was too much for him.

"Belzer," Geof replied. I decided that was the fellow's last name, and not some arcane police greeting. He said to me, "You sure you want to stay, Jenny? This could take a good long while."

"I'm sure." I opened the door of a 1952 two-tone blue Chevy and sat on the front seat. Geof followed me and leaned against the car's back window.

"Wonderful old car," I remarked, killing time. I stroked the cloth shoulder of its front seat. "What's it in for?"

Geof smiled. "It was an accessory to a felony. Claims not to have known why it was waiting at the curb when the liquor store was robbed. We're hoping it will turn state's evidence."

I patted the car's dashboard. "Well, be gentle with her. With an understanding judge and a good probation officer, she might yet be rehabilitated."

The mechanic appeared again. This time, with an air of finality and satisfaction, he wiped his hands on a grease rag.

"You can't be done," Geof objected. "You just got started."

"I'm finished." Belzer spoke so softly I had to strain to hear him. "It's the brakes."

Geof gave me a knowing look, and said, "Failed?"

"You could say that," Belzer replied, and smiled at the floor. "You better look at 'em."

Geof examined the car where the mechanic told him to. When he looked back at Belzer, both pairs of police eyes held knowing expressions. "I'll be damned," Geof breathed. "So that's how it was, Belzer. Jenny, come look at this."

I looked where he pointed.

"What am I looking at?" I said, feeling abysmally ignorant.

"The brake line," Geof said.

"There's a hole in it," I observed.

"All his brake fluid drained out of that hole, Jenny," Geof said. "That's why his brakes went out on him."

I peered more closely at the aperture, then caught my breath.

"Yes," Geof said. "It was cut."

I came out from under the car and stared at the two men. "You're saying somebody did this on purpose, that he died because somebody tampered with his brakes and they failed just when he was driving down that hill toward the ocean. But there's no way somebody could know that would happen, is there? I mean, how would the person who did it know the brake fluid would all run out just when Reich happened to be on a hill which just happened to lead to the bay? It's not possible to predict a thing like that, is it? It seems to me those brakes might have failed at any time, not just at that one particular time. Hell, Geof, they might have gone out on him at a stop sign, or when he was driving on a flat road, or even in his own driveway. Isn't that true?"

"Yes," Geof said, and Belzer nodded.

"So it would not necessarily have resulted in his death," I continued. "He might not even have been injured. Am I right, or not?"

"You're right," Geof agreed. "It might have been a practical joke that went terribly wrong."

"Practical joke," said Belzer unexpectedly. "Ha."

"Or," Geof continued, "it might have been someone who wanted to scare Reich for some reason. Maybe we'll get a rash of these incidents and we'll find out that some garage in town is staging brake failures to drum up business."

"I'll ignore that pun," I said, and Belzer grinned at the floor.

Geof smiled. "It wouldn't be the most amazing thing I'd ever seen, you know. At any rate, whatever the cause of the brakes failing, the final effect is the same."

"Homicide," I said.

"Sure. He's dead, whether somebody meant to kill him or not. If they didn't, the only difference will be in the nature and severity of the charges we bring against them."

"You may have other charges to bring against them, too," I suggested. "In the last twenty-four hours, the foreman of the project is killed, the project itself is torched, and somebody slashes the tires on the builder's vehicles. Murder, arson and vandalism. I get the feeling somebody has a grudge against Liberty Harbor!"

"Looks that way," Geof said, "although you'd be the first to tell me how, supposedly, everybody loves the place."

"Still, it's a whale of a lot of coincidence that these events occurred on the same weekend—when the harbor has no previous record of any trouble at all."

"Well, we will investigate them as separate incidents, with an eye toward linking them. All we need is a motive," he said ruefully. "All we need is to find somebody who *doesn't* love Liberty Harbor."

"He ought to stand out," I said, "like black on white."

But Geof had turned back to the young mechanic. "Good work, son," he said. "I'll send Ailey Mason down to get your full workup. Make it fast, will you?"

"Yes, sir."

Geof put a hand under my elbow to steer me toward the door. I smiled a goodbye at Belzer, but he didn't notice. He was lovingly stroking the chassis of the '52 Chevy, sharing his moment of glory with something that would understand.

The door closed behind us. We stood once more in the stairwell.

"Son?" I said.

"He brings out the paternal in me, I guess." Geof paused,

started to say something, paused again. "For lack of some-one shorter and whiter who looks like me."

I stared at his back as he led the way upstairs.

Well, I thought, here's a new twist: children.

But I said nothing, acutely aware of his awareness of my saying nothing. At the first landing, I tugged at the bottoms of his swim trunks. "This being homicide," I said, "I won't be seeing much of you for a while."

He stopped, turned and looked down at me.

"Know one of the things I love most about you? About our, for lack of a better word, relationship?"

I shook my head.

"I like it that I'm going to be gone days and nights until we solve this Reich business, or don't solve it. And that you'll miss me, but not much."

"Some men would be insulted by that."

"Some men are little boys who still want to be the center of Mommy's universe. It gives me a fine free feeling to know you can live without me." His smile grew lopsided. "Whether or not I could live without you, though, that's a question to which this detective does not have a clue."

"Well, that's one case we don't have to solve today."

He leaned down, gripping my shoulders and pulling me toward him. He pressed my head against his belly; I felt the damp heat of his body through his shirt. He said, pulling me up to a higher step so that my face was closer to his, "But when this is over, Jenny, then we face it. I mean it. I'm not willing to play house with you forever. I want to make a home."

He kissed me. I returned it forcefully.

We drew apart. "I thought I already had my answer last night," he said, "but that kiss makes me wonder if you know your own mind."

"It is," I admitted, "sometimes a stranger to me."

But I had nothing more to say then. When he saw that was the case, he turned and recommenced our silent trek back to his office.

chapter
8

On Monday, I returned to the more mundane, but more immediately rewarding world of Foundation work.

When I walked into the office, I found my staff gathered around that morning's paper, which contained the first printed word of the weekend's death and destruction. Faye Basil's expression was maternal, concerned. "Jenny," she said, "are you all right?" I assured them all that I was. My assistant director, Derek Jones, wanted to know who killed Reich, as if I were privy to secret information. "Do the police know something they're not telling?" Derek demanded.

"If they do," I said, "they're not telling me, either."

"Why would anybody want to harm the project?" asked Marvin Lastelic, our part-time controller. He looked hurt, as would many people in this town when they considered that same question. "It's a good thing for everybody!"

"I don't know, Marv."

The paper headlined: HARBOR PROJECT SABOTAGED, with a subhead that read like my own thoughts: *Foreman Killed, Buildings Ablaze, and Vandalism Spell Trouble for Renova-*

tion. The first paragraphs detailed Reich's plunge into the bay and the subsequent discovery of the slice in his brake line. Inside, there was a full-page spread of photographs from the groundbreaking.

"There's you with the Reverend Eberhardt." Faye Basil pointed at one of the pictures. Hardy and I grinned at each other as at some private joke, all hair, teeth and eyeballs. She said, "My, he's nice-looking."

"Here's the one I like." Derek chuckled. He pointed to a group picture that had been snapped at the exact moment when our committee fully comprehended the magnitude of the danger roaring toward us. It was funny, if inadvertently so. The photographer must have shot it seconds before he dropped his camera on the pier and joined the committee in our dive for safety. (One of the humorous ironies of that afternoon had been the anguish of the press corps who'd been *in* the news for once—while most of their equipment floated uselessly to the bottom of the bay. "Up a creek with a Pentax," as one camerawoman had mourned.) There we all were, all ten of us: one face was openmouthed in disbelief; another was dumb with shock; a third looked as if the devil himself were approaching in a pickup truck. As for me, if there had been a caption above my head, it would have read, "Oh shit."

Derek's finger moved down to a photograph of the police bringing Reich's truck back up to the surface of the bay. "Jeez," he said, and whistled. "When we promise publicity for the groundbreaking of Liberty Harbor, we deliver."

"Jenny," Faye interrupted, "the media are after you, I'm afraid. There are messages for you to call the Port Frederick *Times,* WKYZ, WNAB . . ." She held up a sheaf of pink slips and waved them under my nose. "And a couple of papers in Boston, or maybe they were TV stations . . ."

"They want to interview you as an eyewitness," Marvin Lastelic said proudly. Marv was the oldest one of us on the Foundation staff; he was honest, loyal and dedicated. "I looked for you on the morning news shows, but I couldn't find you."

"I skipped town, Marvin."

"So how is the detective?" Derek, ever impudent, grinned.

"Busy," I said repressively. "As we all should be. Faye, I'll take those messages now." As I flipped through them, I had an odd sensation that my staff was holding its collective breath. Then I came to the last pink slip. "Oh Lord," I groaned. "My father called."

They exchanged glances they meant to be discreet. It was no secret that James Damon Cain III was contentedly living out his forced retirement in Palm Springs, on the fat of the trust funds his father had left him and which the company bankruptcy had not touched.

"Did he say what he wants?" I asked Faye.

Again, those discreet glances that should have told me something.

"Uh," said Faye.

"What?" I demanded. "What?"

"He's here, Jenny," Derek said.

"Here?" My voice rose in dismay. "In Poor Fred?"

"No . . ." Faye's hazel eyes drifted toward the closed door of my office. "He's here now . . . in your office."

"Oh God, give me strength," I moaned.

On cue, as if he'd been listening—which I doubted since my father had never really grasped the fact that entire hemispheres of people proceeded with their lives in his absence—his remarkable face appeared around the door. It was a deeply tanned face framed by a movie-star sweep of silver hair that brushed the collar of his open-neck golf shirt. You'd have sworn this was the American ambassador to the Court of St. James, or Cary Grant's twin brother. I'd known strangers to walk up and ask for his autograph, just because he looked as if he ought to be famous.

He was famous, all right, at least in Port Frederick.

Death and arson faded from my mind as I faced the more immediate dangers posed by the walking, talking disaster I called "Dad."

"Jennifer, my dear," he said, "how lovely to see you!"

Faye, despite all she knew about him, sighed.

I slumped within my sophisticated executive suit. I felt

shrunken to ten years old again, and wishing my beautiful father would recognize my existence apart from his own. If he knew what I'd been through that weekend, he didn't give a clue.

"Hi, Dad," I said, thoroughly depressed. "How's tricks?"

We pecked cheeks.

He followed me into my office and took the chair across from my desk. He'd never seen me at work before, but he didn't comment on that, either.

"I nearly drowned this weekend, Dad," I said ruthlessly. "And then I was nearly incinerated."

"Were you?" He brightened as if I'd said a particularly clever thing. "Well, you're looking fine now, dear. Do you know, there is no decent accommodation in this godforsaken burg? I've had to resort to a Ramada, if you can believe it."

"How awful for you."

"They don't even turn down the bed linens at night!" He shook his gorgeous head over the slovenliness, not to mention the sheer inconsiderateness of it all. "I'm so glad I didn't bring your stepmother."

One small step for mankind, I thought ungraciously.

"And how is your mother?" He was unaware of the incredible tactlessness in his conversational juxtaposition of the two women, one of whom he'd left for the other. "Is she doing well, Jennifer?"

"As well as can be expected," I said in a dead-steady voice, "when one is comatose most of the time."

"Good, good." With my father, you were never sure if you were part of the conversation, because he never actually replied to anything that was said to him, but just carried on wherever his ephemeral mind led him. It was a lovely land my father inhabited, and one where no one else was admitted. He said, "Well, I thought I'd drop by Jack Fenton's office at the bank this afternoon and offer my assistance."

"I beg your pardon?"

"They'll want the family to be part of it, of course," he

said, as if I hadn't spoken. I hadn't the faintest idea what he was going on about. "And I do have all that valuable experience with major building projects."

"Major building projects?" I stared at him. "You mean the canning plant you had built that threw us into bankruptcy? Is that the valuable experience you're talking about, Dad?"

"Of course, dear." He smiled, taking from my question only those words he chose to hear. "They'll want me for an advisor of sorts, I expect. I'm a bit surprised I haven't heard from Jack before this."

"Dad?" I waited until I thought I had his eye. "What are you talking about, Dad?"

The fine gray eyes drifted toward the window and out to sea again. "They might have named it Cain Harbor," he said with an unmistakable trace of miff. "The plant was just up the road, after all, and the family has been awfully important to this town."

"You can say that again." And if *he* didn't, all those employees he had betrayed would. I was beginning to get a familiar sinking feeling that I associated only with my father. With a sense of dread, I said, "You're not talking about Liberty Harbor, are you?"

"Such a meaningless name, no connection to history at all," he replied, conveniently ignoring three hundred years of black struggle. "Now Cain Harbor . . . that has some snap!"

"Snap," I said like a stunned parrot. "Dad, you haven't come back just to get involved with Liberty Harbor . . . have you? Is that what you're saying?"

His eyes focused for a brief instant.

"Of course," he said petulantly. "I wish you'd pay attention, Jennifer. They'll need the backing of some of the more influential families, don't you know. It seems to me a small thing I can do for my hometown."

"Noblesse oblige," I murmured, reeling.

"I want you to get the press on the phone," my father said firmly, as if they were one entity with one telephone. "And let them know that Jimmy Cain is back in town!"

I couldn't speak. It was all I could do not to laugh hysterically. As I struggled to maintain sobriety, he gazed benignly out the window, smiling to himself at some private amusement. And suddenly I felt protective toward this loopy person who was my father. No way would I deliver him into the hands of reporters to whom he would be tasty front page copy. I could see the headlines: CALAMITY CAIN RETURNS! No, he and the town must be spared that ordeal. Besides, if he made the papers again, my sister would go bonkers, and that would further complicate my life.

"Dad." I was brilliantly inspired. "As long as you're here, how would you like to stay on a boat?"

He seemed to think it over.

"Is it a nice one?" my father said.

At that moment, Faye put through a phone call from Webster Helms, the project architect.

"Jenny!" His voice, always reedy, was registering on this day in the higher ranges of hysteria. "I've called an emergency meeting of the advisory committee. My office. Conference Room. Two o'clock."

"Okay," I said.

"Got to nip this in the bud!"

"Fine."

While she had me, Faye put through another call.

"Thought you'd like to know," Geof said in evident disgust, "that thanks to the shortsightedness of yours truly, Belzer got his own fingerprints all over Reich's truck. It's useless to us in that way now."

"Um."

"Jenny, are you there?"

"Sure."

"You sound preoccupied. What's going on down there that's more engrossing than murder?"

"I don't believe you've met my father," I said.

The next call was one I made, and with it I got Dad fixed up with a place to stay that was more to his liking. The *Amy Denise* was no billionaire's yacht, but it was nicely appointed for a boat its size. Even though there would be no one to turn down his sheets at night, the idea of staying on a boat offered just enough social cachet, with a hint of daring, to tickle my father's fancy. Furthermore, Ted Sullivan professed delight at having a guest aboard to look after his boat for a while.

"I hope it will be a short while," I told Ted.

"I'm sure you do," he said with full understanding. "Just keep me posted as to where he takes her."

"I will, Ted."

But what to do in the meantime with my dad?

"Derek!"

His trim blond head appeared in my office doorway.

"Drive my father to the bank, will you?" I said. "And *personally* escort him to Jack Fenton's office." If anyone could keep Jimmy Cain out of trouble for the rest of the day, the banker could.

"Gotcha," said Derek, with a knowing nod.

Finally, I was able to turn to Foundation business. For the first time since Friday morning, life seemed a little more under control.

chapter
9

It continued to seem so until later that day at the emergency meeting of the Liberty Harbor Advisory Committee.

As we all stood around before the meeting, telling war stories about the previous Saturday, Betty and Pete Tower served hors d'oeuvres.

"But this is a business meeting, Betty," Webster Helms protested. He lifted from the tray a chunk of charcoal-broiled seafood that was mated to a hunk of canned pineapple on a toothpick. Webster eyed it with distaste. He said, "You don't serve hors d'oeuvres at a business meeting, for heaven's sake."

"These hors d'oeuvres *are* business, Webster," Betty Tower snapped back. Betty still sported the French roll, ruffled blouses and tight skirts of the 1950s; she looked like a homecoming queen with a lot of miles on her. Her rotund husband affected stark black suits and starched white shirts, like the Parisian restaurateur he fancied himself to be. Betty said, "We're thinking of serving them at the café. Oh, for God's sake, eat it, Webster. It's dead, it won't bite you."

He chewed it, then swallowed.

"It's lobster," Pete Tower informed us, beaming proudly. "From our lobster pound at the harbor."

At that unappetizing little piece of news, Webster Helms turned ashen. And Ted Sullivan quickly withdrew the hand he had extended toward the tray. Goose Shattuck, who had already taken one of the pineapple and lobster concoctions, stabbed the air with it and boomed, "You think I'll eat from that filthy pound? It's bad enough to smell it every day in this miserable weather. When you gonna clean the damn thing out?"

"Don't you start on us again, Goose," Betty snapped, growing red in the face and leaning angrily toward him. The hors d'oeuvres slid dangerously close to the far edge of the tray. I slipped a hand under it to prop them up and when she didn't notice, slid the entire tray away from her. She was saying loudly to Goose, "We will clean *our* pound next spring when the café is ready to open, and not one minute earlier, do you read me? We've got shedders in that pound, and they'll stay there until they're ready to sell, and that's that!"

Betty tended to rile easily.

"Now honey," her husband murmured ineffectually.

"Here!" Goose stuck the hors d'oeuvres under Ted Sullivan's nose. "You're the great defender of free enterprise, Sullivan—you eat the filthy damn thing!"

Ted looked surprised, but he took the offering before Goose could impale him with it. He said mildly, "But Goose, all I ever said was that it's their property, and they ought to be able to do what they . . ."

"All right, folks!" called Mary Eberhardt from across the room. In her trim beige suit, she looked every inch the minister's wife. As such, I suspected she had long experience in deflecting trouble wherever it arose. And this meeting was already in trouble. I could feel sides forming, even before we'd named the game.

"Everyone is here but the mayor," Mary called out. "But we can't wait forever for her . . . you know how slow those Republicans are to move on anything new!"

A good-natured chuckle circled the room, breaking the ill-temper that was building. Or so I thought. We moved obediently to the table. I caught Ted Sullivan making an unobtrusive deposit in a wastebasket on his way; he winked at me when the hors d'oeuvre hit the bottom of the basket with a plunk. The nine of us who were present sat down, gravitating naturally toward the people with whom we usually voted: Mary and Hardy Eberhardt, Jack Fenton, Ted Sullivan and I filled one side; Goose Shattuck, Betty and Pete Tower, and Webster Helms occupied the other, with a chair reserved for the mayor. I put the Towers' hors d'oeuvres tray in the center of the table. There were lookers, but no takers.

In the absence of our chairwoman, Barbara Schneider, Web Helms rose to start the meeting.

"I have asked you here today," he said, and Hardy Eberhardt nudged me under the table so that I had to bite my lip to keep from smiling, "to address the fact that a party or parties unknown is trying to sabotage Liberty Harbor."

"Oh, come on, Web," Hardy objected. The minister's square black hands were spread out in front of him on the table. "It was just some kids with a bow and arrow, that's all."

"That was no kid who killed Ansen Reich," Goose said heatedly. "And what about my tires, Reverend? How do you explain how somebody just happened to disable me so I couldn't make my usual late rounds?"

"There! You see?" Web Helms pounded a small fist on the polished walnut. "These are clearly acts of sabotage!"

Betty Tower gasped theatrically. "My God," she exclaimed, "it's a maniac!" Her husband clicked repeatedly like castinets.

In spite of their expressions of dismay, however, I sensed a curious lack of spontaneity from the contingent across the table. There was an air in that room of something having been rehearsed. What were they up to? I wondered.

"Hold on." Hardy silenced the hubbub. "I don't believe there's evidence to link the murder with the arson, or with the vandalism of your property, Goose. Is there, Jenny?"

My connection to Geof made me the resident police authority wherever I went. "Not directly," I said, "yet."

"There." Hardy was caustic. "I suggest we refrain from jumping to melodramatic conclusions like some newspapers I could name. Anyway, we have other important matters to discuss today." I saw a look pass between the minister and his wife. But Web Helms interrupted before they could say whatever was on their minds.

"More important things?" Webster heard Hardy incorrectly, either by accident or by choice. "They destroyed my office at the site! They burned my most important blueprints, they . . ."

"Office?" I couldn't help but interject. "Come on, Web, it was just a shack. And you have copies of everything you lost, don't you? Well, don't you?"

"Of course, Jenny, but . . ."

"So," Hardy moved in quickly, "let's not make any more of this than there is. Let's talk about positive things, like . . ."

Betty Tower said sharply, "Well, it's all very well for you to be sanguine about murder and arson, Reverend. I mean, you don't have to preach out there at the harbor, do you? Pete and I have to work there with some murderer running loose!"

"Tsk," her husband said.

Jack Fenton cleared his throat. It was all the distinguished banker ever needed to do to get the attention of any group. "Betty," he said kindly, "the idea of sabotage presupposes the idea of someone with ill feelings against the renovation. And we know how supportive this community is of the project. I simply can't think of anyone who would do such a thing."

"But . . ." sputtered Betty and Webster.

"And it seems to me," the banker continued implacably, "that as the advisory committee for the community, it behooves us to take a calm and conservative point of view."

There was a moment of rebellious silence from across the

table while Betty, Pete, Goose and Web tried to figure out how to regain the conservative label that Jack had so neatly, and mischievously usurped from them.

Webster couldn't handle it.

"I don't care what you say!" he declared passionately. "That maniac was coming right at us! He was trying to kill us! And it's all part of a plot against the harbor!"

Hardy, inadvisedly, grinned. "A Communist plot, Web?" he asked.

"Well," said Ted Sullivan just before Web Helms exploded into a thousand red-haired pieces, "what do you want to do about it, Webster?"

The architect looked at the realtor gratefully.

"A citizens' committee," he blurted, "to patrol and protect the interests of the good citizens of Port Frederick."

"A vigilante committee?" Mary Eberhardt said in dismay. "You can't be serious, Webster. You don't mean guns and all, do you?"

"Second the motion," said Betty Tower.

"What motion?" I said.

"Discussion," commanded Webster.

"I'm for it!" announced Goose, shaking our fillings. "I can let my guards go; God knows, as low as I bid to get this job, I can stand to cut some corners. I say yea!"

"All in favor," Webster said, "say aye."

"Aye," echoed Betty, Pete, Goose and Ted.

"Discussion!" Hardy Eberhardt shouted. "Discussion!"

"All opposed, say nay."

"No!" said Hardy, Mary, Jack and Jenny. "No!"

"As chairman," Web said, "I break the tie by voting affirmatively. Motion carries five to four." And he sank back into his chair and heaved a huge sigh.

"You can't *do* that!" Jack Fenton drew himself up as if every banker's inch of him was outraged. "You can't."

Betty Tower's smile was nearly a smirk. "We've already done it, Jack. Web here is the head of the Citizens' Watch Committee, and I'm second-in-command, and we've got our patrols all lined up for the month. It's a favor to Goose, really, because it allows him to let his guards go, so he'll save all sorts of money that could be better spent at the project. And we citizens will take a more personal interest in keeping the project safe from harm; we're bound to be more effective than paid mercenaries."

"Mercenaries?" I said.

"We didn't have to take a vote at all," she said magnanimously. "We only brought it up in committee today to be gracious; didn't want you folks to feel left out of something that is bound to be important to the project."

"Gracious?" I said.

"Left out?" Hardy said, and then he began to laugh. "The Port Frederick Goddamned Posse!" He pulled a white handkerchief from his suit pocket and wiped his eyes. "Oh, my."

"Now Hardy," his wife murmured. Mary Eberhardt looked shocked, but whether at her husband's language or the foolishness of the motion on the floor, I didn't know. But she held the floor while she had it. "While we're taking votes on one thing and another," she said, so nonchalantly that I turned to stare at her, "there's something that Hardy and I would like the committee to consider."

"Yeah, Web," Hardy sighed, and gave his eyes a last swipe. "After this vigilante business, you owe us one, babe."

"Let's wait for Barbara," Ted Sullivan suggested.

"No," Mary said so quickly I knew something was up. What did they want to vote on that they didn't want Barbara to hear? More tactfully, Mary added, "Let's not wait. We don't want to take up any more of your valuable time than we have to, do we, dear?"

The merriment had gone from her husband's intense brown eyes. In their depths, I thought I glimpsed something angry. And sly.

So we didn't wait for the mayor.

And that's how the Eberhardts managed to get through committee the proposal that would come back tragically to haunt them.

SAY NO TO MURDER

"We propose," said Mary, softly but firmly, "a memorial to the African-Americans who lost their lives in the slave trade which flourished at Liberty Harbor. We, that is the black community of Port Frederick, are thinking of a memorial that we would call the Unmarked Grave . . ."

chapter 10

"The Unmarked Grave?"

Barbara Schneider, our mayor and chairwoman, stood at the far end of the conference table looking at all of us as if we had lost our minds. She'd arrived in time to hear the news, but too late to cast the deciding vote against the proposal.

"At a shopping mall?" she exclaimed. It is difficult to look seriously outraged in a Lilly Pulitzer dress, but Barbara was succeeding. "I never heard of anything so macabre in all my life!"

Everyone else seemed to have been struck dumb by the vehemence of her opposition, so I spoke up. "As you know perfectly well, Barbara, Liberty Harbor is not just a mall. There's the cultural center, and the ship-building school, and . . ."

"And now, friends and neighbors, a gravestone!"

"No, not a gravestone," I corrected her. "That's the point, Barbara. The idea that Hardy and Mary proposed and that we approved is to dig a single grave and leave it unmarked, just as all those thousands of slaves were buried in un-marked graves throughout the country."

"Well, if it's not marked," she said with icy sarcasm, "how is anybody going to know it's there?"

Hardy Eberhardt answered her, not bothering to hide the amusement and triumph in his voice. "There will be a low fence around the grave, and a plain white cross on the grave."

"A cross," she said bitterly. "Oh that's wonderful. Tour-ists will think it's a memorial to a traffic accident."

"No." Mary Eberhardt sighed. "No, Barbara, there will be a few simple words on a small plaque that will be attached to the *small* fence. It will be unobtrusive, I assure you, and we think it will be a lovely tribute."

"But at a shopping center!" The mayor shook her hand-some head in dismay; the movement disturbed not a hair of her perfect coiffure. "It's in dreadful taste!"

"So was slavery," I said.

"You've gone too far this time, Reverend," she intoned. "My Lord, we gave you the employment quota, we gave you space in the mall for your people to set up shops, we even gave you the *name* of the place! And now you trivialize it over something that is merely symbolic instead of real. And just when it was all going so well for you people."

"Us," I said.

"Us?" She turned toward me again as toward an annoy-ing, biting insect.

"That's the problem," I said. "Thinking of them as them and us as us."

"Spare me the polemics, Jennifer," she said coldly. She turned back to stare at Hardy. "What will you want next, Reverend, a memorial restroom marked Coloreds Only?"

Even Betty Tower drew in her breath at that one. But Hardy only laughed that full-bellied laugh of his and said, "Sorry, your Honor, but we got the votes on this one. That'll teach you to get to meetings late."

"I would have been here on time," she said furiously, glaring at Webster Helms at the other end of the table, "if

someone had given me the correct time for the meeting."
But she wasn't to be sidetracked from the Unmarked Grave.
"I am mayor today because I campaigned last time on a
platform of economic recovery, Reverend, and I will not
allow you or anybody else to turn our recovery into a
sideshow for pet causes and special-interest groups."

Hardy continued to smile pleasantly. He'd been weaned
on the civil rights movement of the sixties, and was not
likely to be easily intimidated by a small-town mayor who
didn't like his liberal ideas. So far, Hardy had bested
Barbara in every battle over fair employment and equal
opportunities. Sometimes I worried that in so doing, he
might be losing a bigger war he didn't know he was fighting.
On a personal level, Barbara was a nice enough lady, but on
a political level, she was a fierce opponent who held grudges
that made East and West Germany look like pals. If he had
asked my advice, which he hadn't, I might have told him to
let her win one now and then, just enough small points to
keep her ambition at bay.

"And I'll tell you something, Reverend." Her intelligent
eyes narrowed, as if in sudden inspiration. "The people will
agree with me. They won't let anything stand in the way of
the benefits they'll gain from this renovation. If you don't
believe me, we'll ask them!"

"You want to take it to the people?" Hardy leaned
forward, and his smile turned, wicked. There was an electricity in the air that fairly made my skin crackle. "I'll go
you one better, your Honor. How about taking it to *my*
people, as you would put it? This Sunday, my church, my
pulpit. Winner takes all."

Her mouth fell open slightly, showing small, perfect teeth.
Then she leaned forward avidly to meet him. "Let me get
this straight. You convince the congregation that the grave is
a brilliant idea, and you get it, right? But if I convince them
that it's counterproductive, there will be no grave, no cross,
no more of this memorial nonsense. Right?"

He looked around the table at each of us. "Any objections
from the committee?" he asked. Nobody spoke. "All right,"
he said, turning back to the mayor. "All *right.*"

"You're on, Reverend," said the mayor of Port Frederick, Massachusetts. She wheeled on her heels and clicked off toward the door. But then she paused to wither the temporary chairman with a look. "As for your Citizens' Watch Committee, Webster, that's the second worst idea I ever heard. For God's sake, try not to shoot yourself in the foot."

Our mayor swept out, leaving her fellow conservatives openmouthed with embarrassment. Webster Helms took the yellow pencil on the table in front of him and snapped it neatly in two.

We adjourned shortly thereafter. I walked out of the meeting beside our friendly neighborhood banker, Jack Fenton. "I get the feeling," I said quietly to him, "that we have just been railroaded by two trains coming from different directions."

"This committee has always been home to divergent views," he mused, "but heretofore, we have been able to conduct our debates in a more or less harmonious fashion. And certainly within the privacy of the conference chamber, rather than resorting to public brawls such as the reverend and the mayor have proposed! From where do you suppose this tension stems, this business of friend voting against friend, of open warfare? Do you suppose the troubles at the harbor have put us on edge?"

"Murder will do that," I said dryly. "But never mind about this committee, Jack . . . what have you done with my father?"

"I sent him to lunch with a vice-president of the trust department."

"You have something against this particular VP?"

He smiled. "That is what vice-presidents are for, Jennifer, to assume the more onerous duties the chairman wishes to avoid. My goodness, but your father is certainly put out that we didn't name the harbor after him!"

"You didn't tell him about this meeting?"

He shot me a horrified look. "I didn't get to this age by being stupid," he pointed out.

"Silly of me even to suggest it. But what did you say to his offer to help us with the project?"

The old banker drew himself up to his full and considerable height. "I told your father," he said with dignity, "that he could be of estimable service to the community of his birth by taking Ted Sullivan's boat and anchoring it out in the bay where he could watch over the construction of Liberty Harbor day and night."

"You didn't."

"I did. And I further told him that we would receive his regular reports with all the interest they so richly deserve."

"That," I said, stunned into admiration, "is brilliant."

He squeezed my shoulder paternally, then said in a gentler tone, "He'll be all right, Jennifer, if he can get over this obsession with the harbor. Your father always lands on his feet."

"I don't know that I'd call it an obsession, Jack."

"It would take no less than that to draw your father away from his golf game," he retorted dryly. "I think he views this as an opportunity to vindicate himself with this town." He eyed me. "And his daughters."

"Sherry and me?" I laughed ruefully. "I'm sorry to sound disrespectful, Jack, but my father believes that his very existence is vindication enough for anything."

He didn't argue. When we reached the front door of the building, he said, "I'll see you this Sunday, my dear." And he winked. "At the First Church of the Risen Christ. Oh my, I wouldn't miss this spectacle for anything—even if the Fed offered to lower the prime rate."

Betty and Pete Tower followed us out the door, then passed us. She held her hors d'oeuvres tray far out in front of her chest, and her pert nose in the air. She wasn't being haughty. After our three-hour meeting, the lobster-pineapple treats smelled like a hot day at an old pier.

chapter
11

It was late that evening by the time I got my dad settled on the *Amy Denise*.

"It's awfully small," he said doubtfully.

We stood side by side at the marina, looking up at the boat on which we'd just stowed his luggage. Now there is only a tiny, privileged minority of people in this world who might consider a forty-two-foot pleasure craft to be small, but Jimmy Cain was one of them. I had anticipated the objection, however, and I was ready for him.

"Yes, Dad, so it's easy to handle."

"There's no crew?"

I swallowed an exasperated retort.

"You'll have privacy, Dad."

"But she only does twelve knots," he complained in the same tone in which a child on Christmas morning might say, "But I didn't get my train!"

"She may be slow, but she's steady." Like a salesman who knew his mark, I closed in for the kill. "Great missions from small beginnings grow," I intoned, making up epigrams on the spot. "Great men reap what humble seeds they sow."

My father straightened his shoulders and gazed off into the distance. "How terribly profound," he breathed. "Shakespeare?"

"Jabberwocky."

But he was lost in his dreams of strong men and high purpose. "Well," he said firmly, "I'll be off then, my dear, to Liberty Harbor to do my duty as a citizen."

"Don't dock there," I warned him. "You're doing this privately, you know, so we don't want to advertise your purpose."

"Jennifer," he said with great dignity, "you don't have to tell me my business. I'll let down anchor in the bay, but I'll be able to see everything that goes on . . ."—he waved his binoculars at me—"without anyone knowing what I'm up to." Evidently he thought of himself as a consumer watchdog, Ralph Nader with a tan.

I stood on the dock and waved him off to Liberty Harbor. As he finally pulled away, with a great fanfare of tooting horns and revving engines, I had the psychic feeling of wiping my hands together and sighing, "Whew."

I drove to Geof's house, where we'd been living while he tried to sell it. It was an ugly ultramodern, left over from the second marriage. That wife, Melissa, had left him because she got lonely being married to a cop who was rarely home. She married her lover, a computer whiz with an office in the basement. I wondered, having known a few computer whizzes, if a man couldn't seem just as distant one flight down as he could at police headquarters. The first wife, Roberta, had a career of her own; she had not objected to his physical absence; it was his mental absence when he was in the same room that she objected to. I asked him once, "When is a cop not a cop?" To which he replied, "When he's dead."

Instead of pulling into the garage, I parked in the driveway. I wanted to roll down the window, listen to the grass grow, and savor the solitude. The house, which must have been designed by an architect with a cold heart, was dark. Its owner was working late on the Ansen Reich case.

I thought of Annie Reich.

What was it like in her strange house this night? By now, she knew that her husband had been killed either by mistake or on purpose. How did she feel? Surprised, saddened, outraged? Did she feel anything? Would she, like a goddess, shriek, rend her clothes, tear her hair? No, the image was impossible. More likely, she'd merely drink an extra glass of iced tea. Sweetened.

I fixed myself a supper of leftover vichyssoise and a chicken salad on a croissant, accompanied by a nice, light Riesling wine. A young, female, upwardly mobile repast if ever there was one. The only things missing were a cold pasta salad and a side of quiche.

The wine made me sleepy, so I fixed a cup of coffee, then curled up in bed between piles of grant applications and corporate reports. For a half hour, I sorted through the applications, eliminating the obvious losers . . . "No," I said to six applicants whose projects extended beyond the town boundaries; "no" to several proposals that would duplicate projects we already funded; "no" to a couple of organizations for whom we would only be throwing good money after bad; "no" to a political action committee who should have known better than to ask; and "no" to a food distribution network that was run by a board of directors that I wouldn't have trusted any further than I could throw a loaf of the stale bread they dispensed.

It's depressing to turn down so many people, some of them deserving. Takes a certain steeling of the heart. I was glad when the phone rang and interrupted me.

"Hello," I said, "Hard-hearted Hannah here."

Geof laughed. "Something tells me you're working late tonight. If you're writing 'NO' in big block letters all over grant applications, I suspect this is not the time to propose."

"Well, you could fill out a form," I said, "and I could present your proposal to our board of trustees."

"Yeah, but they always go by your recommendation. What would you tell them on this one?"

"I'd tell them it was held up in committee, pending

on-site investigation and that we ought, perhaps, to weigh the alternatives."

"They weigh heavily," he said, "on my mind."

"I'll wait up for you."

"Better not, it's going to be a late one." In his pause, I sensed frustration. "You know, from the way you described Ansen Reich to me, I pictured the man having more enemies than Richard Nixon could even imagine."

"Richard Nixon could imagine a lot of enemies."

"But Reich seems to have offended everybody he ever met, without actually causing anyone to hate him. I get the impression he was only annoying, like a mosquito."

"It would have to be an awfully big mosquito," I said doubtfully. "The Mosquito That Ate Chicago."

"Well," he said, "what I'm leading up to is that instead of having too many leads to pursue, and too many suspects, we have too few. Which means, if we can't solve his murder by viewing it as a separate incident, maybe it is related to the other troubles at the harbor."

"So you think it's sabotage."

"I didn't say that."

"But you think the acts are connected?"

"I didn't say that, either."

"I'm not a reporter, Geof. Tell me what you think!"

"I would," he said irritably, "if I could."

"In other words, you don't know."

"You're quick tonight."

I clamped my jaw and waited for an apology.

Finally he said, "You shouldn't ever think that they had no grounds for divorce."

"I'm going to change the subject now," I said.

"I think that's a good idea."

"Geof, some of the members of the Liberty Harbor Advisory Committee have formed something they call the Citizens' Watch. It's a vigilante committee. They plan to patrol the harbor, with guns, I believe."

He swore. "Don't tell me, let me guess: Helms, Shattuck, Tower, Tower and Schneider."

"Schneider wasn't there. Sullivan."

"Ted? What the hell's got into him?"

"He agrees with the rest of them that all this trouble is being caused by somebody who wants to sabotage the project, and I guess he agrees that the police . . . I'm sorry . . . aren't doing enough about it, fast enough."

"I don't suppose," he said caustically, "they have any bright ideas as to who this saboteur might be? Some shopowner, maybe, who didn't get the spot he wanted in the mall? Or how about somebody from the Boston Chamber of Commerce who thinks we're going to steal their tourists?"

I waited a beat. "I, on the other hand, think the police are wonderful."

He laughed. "I'll tell Ailey."

"Mañana," I said.

"Which is more than I deserve," he said, and hung up.

I lifted a corporate report from the pile on the bed and leafed through it. The phone rang again.

Forgetting I wasn't at the office, I said: "Jenny Cain."

"Nigger lover," a voice breathed. "You keep away from that ugly preacher or you'll be the next body in the bay." He branched out from there to describe interracial sexual activities. I hung up on him. At least, I assumed it was a he. The voice was vaguely familiar, which made the call all the more unnerving.

"Damn you," I said to the telephone. I was loath to touch it again, as if the slime might ooze out of the receiver to contaminate me. But I wanted to talk to the one person who could comfort the frightened, results guaranteed. So the disgusting call could not infect my night and ruin it, I looked up a number in my personal directory, and dialed.

"Helping Friends," a gentle voice said clearly and distinctly. It was the suicide center. "My name is Ida. May we help you?"

"Mrs. Basil, please."

"I'm sorry," the young voice said. "We are not allowed to acknowledge the last names of our volunteers."

"All right." I tried a sneak attack from another flank. "May I speak to Faye?"

"Sure," the voice said cheerfully.

"This is Faye," said a motherly voice. "May I help you?"

"It's Jenny," I said, feeling better already. "Why won't they let you give out your last names?"

"Jenny?" She sounded surprised. "It's for our protection. Now and then we receive calls from truly unbalanced people."

"So do I, Faye," I explained.

"That's terrible," she said comfortingly. "But you just don't give it another thought, Jenny. There are some unpleasant people in this world, but we don't have to dwell on them."

I smiled at the now-friendly telephone. Faye had such a life-giving, renewing way about her. If Philly Reich had managed to contact her the night he felt suicidal, he might still be alive. Maybe Faye had been right about that, just as Hardy Eberhardt had been correct in predicting the reaction to our being photographed together.

With her sweet nature, Faye cleansed the phone lines that had been fouled. Before I extinguished the lights in the bedroom, I turned on the phone-answering machine so that filthy-minded bigots could not disturb my dreams.

I slept fine, thank you.

It never occurred to me to wonder if Hardy had received a malignant message, too.

chapter
12

Sunday. We had to park five blocks away from the church to find a space. The mayor's venture into all-black territory was an event the local media had heralded like the second coming. Only this was a first coming.

In the sanctuary, white faces wearing eager-to-please expressions bobbed like marshmallows in chocolate sauce. In short order, I spied every member of the advisory committee and most of the town council. The Democrats looked stunned and suspicious.

I also recognized four plainclothes cops.

"That's offensive," I complained to Geof. He was elegant in summer pinstripes; I was hot in silk. There'd been no more trouble all week, nor any hint of trouble for this day.

"It's meant to be defensive," he said, his eyes scanning the crowd. "You never know what sort of racist nuts an event like this will attract. We could get one of those die-for-Allah crazies, or a ripe banana from the KKK. Eberhardt knows they're here. If he's not offended, why should you be?"

"Are you annoyed with me? Or with white suburban liberals in general?"

He squeezed my hand. "Sorry, it's the cop coming out in me. I don't like to throw firecrackers like Schneider and Eberhardt on the same pile. Somebody might get careless and light a match."

We threaded our way down the crowded aisle. In the front row, Mary Eberhardt waved at me and I waved back. Betty and Pete Tower sat directly behind her, their backs as stiff as hymnals.

"Amazing," I whispered. We excused our way past five pairs of feet and into the center of a pew. "In Pete's and Betty's church, the basic sermon is 'God's in His Heaven, All's White with His World.'"

"I'll be damned," Geof said. "What the hell is she doing here?" An elderly black man in front of us turned around and raised a stern eyebrow at Geof's language. The thirty-four-year-old detective murmured meekly, "Excuse me, sir."

"What's who doing here?" I asked. "Betty? She's on the advisory com—"

"No." He took my chin and swiveled it around toward the back of the church. There in the last row, large and dully white, sat Annie Reich.

But she was not the most eye-catching addition to the church that day, for on the altar where Barbara would speak there hung a wooden cross that looked suspiciously like the one that Hardy and Mary had proposed for the Unmarked Grave.

Oh Hardy, I thought, you sly dog.

Neither painted nor varnished, the cross was obviously of recent and quick construction. Its vertical shaft was about two feet long, the crossbar spanned a foot, and each bar was about four inches wide and an inch across. What gave the game away, however, was the bottom of it which had been whittled to a dull point that would be just right for pounding into the ground. When the mayor spoke, all eyes would be fastened on the *fait accompli* that hung before her.

My eyes, however, were fastened on a procession coming

down the center aisle. It was not the minister and his choir. It was my father, trailed by a photographer and someone who looked terrifyingly like a reporter.

"Oh, my Lord," I breathed, "let us pray."

My father was affecting a grand entrance—all silver hair, tanned face and big smile. As he made his way down the carpet, he nodded at faces he recognized. They stared back at him. A whisper began that rolled along the pews like a wave on the ocean. "Jimmy Cain is back!" "Isn't that Jimmy Cain?" "How dare he show his face in this town!" The reporter looked as if he had died and gone to heaven.

I had merely died, or wished I could.

He didn't see me, which may have had something to do with the fact that I was hunched down in my seat. "What's the matter with you?" Geof asked.

"I was born," I replied.

But I didn't have to leap instantly to my father's rescue because, just as he slid gracefully into a pew toward the front, the organ came to *my* rescue with a crashing chord.

Hardy Eberhardt marched from a side entrance to his pulpit, his blue robes flowing. The force of his presence brought the congregation to silence.

"Brothers and Sisters!" he said into the microphone. "We welcome our visitors this day to the blessed home of the Risen Christ!"

"Amen, Brother Eberhardt!"

"Let us pray," said Hardy, "to the glory of the Lord God Almighty!"

And so we prayed, some of us more fervently than others; and for the next twenty minutes we listened to scripture, we sang roof-raising hymns, we swayed in our pews to the rolling anthems of the choir. And then we sat down again.

Expectantly.

"Brothers and Sisters in the Lord." Hardy began with a near-whisper that forced us to lean forward in our pews. Then with every sentence, he raised the volume and the passion. "Brothers and Sisters, the Lord God brought His children out of Canaan . . ."

"Amen!"

"Out of degradation and deprivation, out of anguish and agony, out of death and destruction, the Lord God delivered His children!"

"Praise God!"

"And His children were grateful unto Him, were they not?"

"Yes, Lord."

"And built Him a temple, did they not?"

"Yes, Lord."

"To the glory everlasting of the Lord God Almighty, His children raised a temple to honor His holy name. And I say unto you this day, you children of that same holy God, I say unto you . . . when the Lord delivers us from evil, it behooves us to bestow all honor upon Him!"

"Thank you, Lord!"

Hardy raised his arms above his head so the blue robes flew like angels' wings. "If the Lord God sees fit in His unquestionable wisdom to bestow the blessings of life everlasting upon us, His children, how shall we honor Him? As a child honors his parents, so shall we honor Him! So shall we build a place upon this Earth where men shall know our suffering, where men shall know our trials, where men shall know the jubilation of our liberation!"

Hardy walked around to the front of the pulpit. He detached the wooden cross and thrust it high above his head and toward the congregation.

"Upon a cross the Lord our God sacrificed His only Son for us! Upon a cross! And the angels rolled away the stone and He rose again!"

"Yes, Lord!"

"Lord, my God." Hardy raised his face to the heavens and closed his eyes. "We will dig a grave in Thy earth. Into that grave we will pour the bitterness of our sufferings. We will cover that bitterness with healing earth! We will mark that grave with the blessed cross of Jesus, the empty cross from which He did descend . . ."

He opened his eyes to stare straight at his congregation.

"We shall mark that grave with the cross from which our

people did also descend forever from the death of slavery! Yes, Lord!"

In the breathless silence, he lowered his arms. Gently, with bent head, he propped the cross lovingly against the pulpit in plain view of all. He stepped back behind the pulpit, leaned into the microphone and said gently, "Brothers and Sisters, I give you the Honorable Mayor of this city, our beloved Sister Barbara Schneider."

Sister Barbara rose from her front-row seat beside Mary Eberhardt, pale with the knowledge that she would never live this down among the more rock-ribbed of her Republican supporters, and realizing that she now had about as much chance of persuading this audience as the Pharaoh's men had when the Red Sea rushed over them.

The congregation stirred briefly again. It was like coming out from under the spell of a master hypnotist; we blinked our eyes at the real world.

Barbara lifted the cross and quietly placed it out of sight behind the pulpit. Gutsy and smart, I thought. She looked out over us, waiting patiently for us to settle down.

"Thank you," she said clearly, graciously, "for welcoming me as your Sister. We are, indeed, a family that is united in our enthusiasm for the great economic revival that Liberty Harbor represents for all of us, black or white, young or old, Republican or Democrat."

The audience murmured in appreciation of that truth; there was even a tentative "Amen" to be heard in the crowd. She was no evangelist, but she was surprisingly effective.

"It is essential," she said, "that every individual part of the project contribute to the success of the whole. Surely there is no one among us who could not agree that the work of building the harbor must proceed at top speed . . ."

"Oh yeah?" came a deep voice from the rear.

Barbara must have thought it was only another "Amen." She was three words into her next sentence before her head jerked up. "What?" said the mayor. "What?"

We in the pews had already whirled our heads to the rear. We watched, with Barbara, as a young white man rose to his feet from the back row. His face, under a Greek fisherman's cap and several days' growth of beard, was gaunt and pale as a poet's; his clothes looked as if they had come from the back of a closet of a 1960s hippie who had outgrown them. His voice was a raspy baritone that sounded as if it hadn't been used in years. He was short and slight, more like a boy than a man.

"You said," he replied to Barbara, "that everybody agrees the renovation should proceed at top speed. And I said, 'Oh yeah.'"

The mayor, who'd handled her share of hecklers, smiled at us to indicate she recognized a lunatic when she saw one. She raised her voice.

"And so . . ." was all she managed.

"The reason I said, 'Oh yeah,'" the young man persisted, topping her in volume, "is that Liberty Harbor is going to come to a complete halt as of right now."

An ominous rumble began deep in the throats of the congregation, uniting black members and white visitors alike.

Hardy bounded to his feet. He shot a quick, commanding glance at the plainclothes cops who started walking, like deacons in a hurry, up the aisle toward the intruder. Beside me, Geof tensed but didn't move.

Barbara continued. "And who, sir, are you?"

"You should have discovered that a long time ago," the young man said with an unpleasant bark of laughter. "My name is Atheneum McGee."

I clutched Geof's arm.

"That's McGee!" the stranger shouted angrily. "As in Lobster McGee, my great-uncle. As in the waterfront property my relatives sold out from under me to your goddamn cheating developers." He thumped his thin chest. "Nobody asked *me* if I wanted to sell *my* property. And I don't! So put that in your harbor and sail it!"

"Atheneum McGee!" Barbara exclaimed. "Aren't you the one who's supposed to be dead?"

"Well, this must be Easter," the old man in front of us said querulously, "'cause that man done resurrected."

A nervous titter ran through the sanctuary.

"You're the great-nephew who died in Vietnam!" Barbara said. "What are you doing *here?*"

"I'm here to get what's mine, lady." Atheneum McGee raised his cap, then crammed it back down on his curls. They were graying, revealing him to be older than he looked at first glance, old enough to have served in Southeast Asia in the sixties or seventies. He began to clamber over the other people in his aisle, as if making for the door. But he was halted in midstride by a full blast of volume from the Reverend Eberhardt.

"Wait!" Hardy thundered. "If you are Atheneum McGee, we can only apologize, for we sincerely believed you to be dead. We have no wish to cheat a rightful heir to Lobster McGee's property.

"Surely, sir . . ." and Hardy's voice turned mellifluous, soothing as a cool hand on a hot brow . . ."surely there is time for men and women of good faith to reason together. Like . . . five minutes from now in my study behind the nave."

Atheneum McGee peered back over his scrawny shoulder like a rat that has just smelled the cheese.

"Bring your checkbook, preacher," he drawled. "I was *real* fond of my great-uncle. That land's got a whole lot of sentimental value to me, you know?"

"I believe it," said Hardy in the same stern tone of voice with which he might have faced the devil. "I do believe it, sir."

"Amen," said the old man in front of us.

chapter
13

Following the world's fastest benediction, Hardy marched his choir down the center aisle at breakneck speed, the mayor at his side. Their differences over the Unmarked Grave temporarily forgotten, they looked united in their common desire to see that nothing interfered with the steady progress of Liberty Harbor.

"The advisory committee meets in my study in five," Hardy barked. Politically, he added, "If you please."

I tried to reach my father, but the congregation was in pandemonium, and I couldn't even see him. I wasn't too worried now, however, because Atheneum McGee had wrested attention from my dad; the reporters and photographers were stampeding to get to the scarecrow in the back row. Every member of the church and visitor, as well, seemed to be shoving to reach Atheneum and to plead with him to be reasonable, and not to obstruct the renovation our town needed so badly. Men who'd been out of work for months tugged at his ratty sleeve; mothers with babies in their arms pushed those babies toward him as proof that Mommy needed work because Baby needed shoes. "Listen fella," Goose Shattuck roared, "we're six months into that job! You want your fair share, don't bug us. Go after those relatives of yours who had you dead and buried!"

Jack Fenton put a hand on Goose's beefy shoulder and said, surprisingly, "Shut up, Goose." The banker said coolly to Atheneum McGee, "If you didn't die in Vietnam, where have you been all this time, Mr. McGee? I wonder if the army might not be interested in that information."

An expression that unpleasantly combined cunning and fear crossed Atheneum McGee's sharp features. "You can't blackmail me into disappearing," he said nastily. "It's not my fault the army identified the wrong dead body! My buddy and me, we was blown up in a cave in Nam. Damn near knocked me into Cambodia, and when I woke up I didn't know my ass from my army. Wandered around in the jungle living off the gooks, didn't even know my name. It was my sergeant, man; he identified my buddy's body, said it was me, said it was my buddy who was MIA. I got witnesses, man! I can prove it."

Again, that image of a rat came to my mind. Atheneum McGee looked like a diseased, crazed rat. Rabid. Vicious. Jack Fenton and the rest of the crowd around him seemed to sense it, too, and backed off, giving him breathing room.

Unexpectedly, Webster Helms took advantage of the moment to rescue McGee by pulling him out of the importuning, hostile crowd and into a room with a lock on it. Just before Web slammed the door, Pete and Betty Tower ran up and Betty pounded on it. "Let us in, Web," Betty said shrilly. "Can't let him delay us, got to keep on schedule!" Web allowed them in, muttering something that sounded like, "Darn fool." I heard the lock fall into place.

That left the rest of us with nothing to do but mill around and wring our hands. Some of the crowd gave up and left for their homes and lunches. I looked futilely for my father, only to give up and head for Hardy's study. But first, I turned to Geof who was still beside me.

"At least this isn't the kind of trouble you feared."

But he was scanning the horizon, looking so bloodhoundish I expected him to sniff the air. "Um," he said, "Excuse me, Jenny." I watched him convene the other cops in a corner of the sanctuary, and then they dispersed to different areas of the church. Geof, feigning that official pose that fools no one, slipped into the crowd on the front steps.

"Come on, Jenny," commanded Mary Eberhardt. "This way."

She had also rounded up Jack Fenton, Goose Shattuck and Ted Sullivan. Mary led us to her husband's office to join the mayor. Ted and I took the only chairs. Jack and Goose paced, crossing paths in the center of the room. Barbara stared out the window.

"Damnedest thing," Jack muttered to the carpet. "If this isn't the damnedest thing."

Betty Tower's blond head appeared in the doorway. She looked flushed, strained, unsteady on her feet as if the day's shock had made her woozy. "Ted," she said, her voice trembling a bit, "take my place in there. If I have to spend five more minutes with that smelly moron, I'll be sick."

Ted left quickly, followed by Goose. Shortly after, Jack Fenton couldn't seem to stand it any longer, and he disappeared, too, along with the mayor. For the next half hour, the minister's office was a giant jack-in-the-box with many heads popping in and out.

"You talk to him, Mary!"

"All right, but don't expect miracles."

"Why not, it's a church, isn't it?"

"Where's Hardy?"

"Gone to phone a lawyer, get some legal advice about this. How come we don't have a lawyer on the committee?"

"Jenny, aren't you going in?"

"No," I said firmly. "Too many cooks."

They came and went, sometimes reporting progress, more often looking discouraged. Atheneum McGee was playing us like a poker hand, knowing all the time that he held the winning ace. "But Ted," I said at one point when the realtor and I were the only people in Hardy's study, "what if he's not really Atheneum McGee?"

"But he is," Ted said. "I'd bet on it."

I shrugged. "Yeah, so would I."

Hardy came back from another trip to the telephone. "Okay," he said, "where's Jack? We need to get some cool heads together to talk to the man again."

"Getting a cup of coffee, I think," I reported. "Who's in there with McGee now?"

"I don't know!" The blue-robed arms flew up in frustration. "If I could get him alone, I could persuade him to see the error of his ways."

"Go team," I said, to which he, to his credit, grinned.

"Hardy." I stopped him before he flew out the door again. "I hate to be the local pessimist, but I don't think all this arm-twisting is worth it. People are so litigious these days; and Atheneum McGee strikes me as a person who will sue everybody who ever had anything to do with the project, whether or not they're responsible for his problems. He'd probably sue the phone company because nobody called him to tell him he's an heir. He'll probably sue the funeral home that buried the wrong body. He'd sue his great-uncle Lobster if he were still alive."

"You," said Mary Eberhardt, who had stuck her head in the door, "are what is known as a wet blanket. Besides, we're making progress, I can feel it."

I shook my head. "That man is after every penny he can get," I said. "If we were turnips he'd squeeze blood from us. I've a feeling this project is going on hold for a good long time, just about as long as it takes him to get an injunction to stop construction, and for us to appeal it, and for him to . . ."

"You're wrong!" Ted Sullivan crowed. Jack Fenton, the Towers and Goose pushed in behind him. "We've got him convinced to leave us alone and to get his money from the other heirs."

"I don't believe it," I said.

"Drip." Mary smiled. "Drip, drip."

"Oh, ye, of little faith," her husband said to me.

"So who's with him now?" Mary looked from face to eager face. They all stared back blankly at her. "Oh, for heaven's sake," said she, the master organizer, "we can't just leave him alone in there to change his mind." She wheeled around to retrieve the heir apparent. I sat in my chair and watched the others congratulate each other for managing to persuade McGee to sue his relatives instead of us.

When she left the room it was eleven minutes past twelve, by the clock on the wall in Hardy's study. At thirteen minutes past twelve a piercing scream shattered the bonhomie.

"Mary!" Hardy said, turning as pale as it was possible for him to turn. "Oh Lord, my Mary!"

We rushed after him, running toward the sound of that horrible scream which continued to echo through the halls of the church. The screaming was, indeed, coming from Mary Eberhardt's throat. But we weren't the first to reach her. Geof was.

We found them both kneeling on the floor of the room in which Webster had sequestered Atheneum McGee. It was the practice and changing room for the choir. In respect for the negotiations that had been going on inside their quarters, the choir had neatly folded their blue robes and piled them on the floor outside the door. But even if they'd been able to hang their pretty robes in the closet, they would not have wished to do so.

Two legs sprawled out of that closet, their feet shod in sandals. The rest of the body lay half in, half out of the closet. It was Atheneum McGee, of course. He lay face-down, his arms flung out above his head. Deep into his back, in the region of his heart, somebody had thrust with violent and hateful force the whittled end of the cross for the Unmarked Grave.

chapter
14

We viewed the corpse from the doorway because Geof had already blocked access with an overturned chair. "Stay there," he directed. "Jenny, take your friends back to Eberhardt's study. Nobody leaves the church. If you see anybody try to leave, stop them. If you can't stop them, call for one of us to do it."

"Let me see my wife," Hardy said urgently. He placed his hands on the chair barrier as if to hurl it out of his way. His eyes were locked on his petite wife who still knelt, softly crying, on the floor near McGee's feet. One of Geof's arms was wrapped around her shoulders; with the other he waved us away.

"Stop right there." Geof's voice was commanding. Hardy hesitated long enough for another policeman to pull him back from that awful room. I began to tug at other sleeves, but to little avail. My fellow committee members were looking at death for the second time in eight days, and they would not be so easily moved.

"I'm all right, darling," Mary Eberhardt said then, as to a frightened child. "You stay there. I'll come to you when they let me. They can't allow you in here, you know that, darling. Fingerprints and all that, I suppose." But then she broke down, again. "Oh Hardy, our cross, our beautiful cross."

His fists clenched at his blue-robed sides, the minister whirled toward the mayor. "You can stop worrying about the Unmarked Grave now, Barbara, can't you? We'll never use that cross . . . it's marked with the blood of murder."

"Hardy," the mayor protested weakly, "you don't think . . . this has nothing to do with . . . I can't believe . . ." She lapsed into a hurt and uncharacteristic silence.

"Sabotage," pronounced Webster Helms. "Murder, fire, vandalism, now another murder."

"All that's lacking," I said wearily, "are plague and pestilence."

He threw me an indignant look. "Well, how else do you explain this, Jennifer? We finally get him to agree to leave us alone and *then* somebody kills him! It's obviously sabotage."

I didn't follow his reasoning, and said so.

As to a slow child, he said, "This murder investigation will impede our work, Jennifer . . ."

"Not my work, it won't," Goose boomed.

Webster ignored the contractor. "And now we may have other heirs to worry about . . . maybe there's a Vietnamese wife someplace, and little slanty-eyed brats."

"Webster," said Jack Fenton sharply, "kindly indulge your bigotry outside of this church."

"But bigotry is the issue," Hardy Eberhardt said, his hot rage having melted down to icy fury. He turned back to Geof. "I received some nasty racist phone calls this week, Bushfield. First time in years. Prompted by those photographs of the groundbreaking that were in the paper." Tactfully, he didn't look at me, but Geof, who knew of my caller, did. The minister said, "You'd better consider the implications of that, in light of this murder weapon."

"Sabotage," said Webster stubbornly.

"Yes," Hardy agreed, "sabotage of the hopes and dreams of the black community in this city."

"We'll consider everything, Mr. Eberhardt," Geof said

impatiently. "Officer Blakemore will now escort all of you back to the study. I said all of you. Now."

"Pete?" Betty Tower suddenly came to life. "Where's Pete?"

Pete, it turned out, was in the men's room throwing up.

It was over an hour later when Geof and his young partner, Ailey Mason, finally joined us in Hardy's study. By then the room was unbearably hot. We'd turned off the ineffectual air conditioner and opened the windows, but that only served to circulate the smoke from Betty's and Ted's cigarettes. "It's like an elevator in here," Goose Shattuck complained more than once. "Put those damn things out."

None of us knew precisely what the police were doing in the choir's chamber while we waited in the pastor's study, but it was easy to guess. We'd all watched television. But whenever any of us tried to discuss it, Pete Tower raised a white handkerchief to his green face, causing Betty to hush us with a sharp rebuke. Mary Eberhardt, who'd been released from that chamber of horror, huddled within her husband's arms. Jack Fenton was erect in a straight-backed chair; he looked as worried as a banker with too many loans outstanding. I stood with the mayor at one of the two windows, trying to find a breeze to breathe. "How could he say that?" Barbara kept whispering to herself. "How could he even think it?"

Now Geof looked at Webster Helms.

"You had him in that room with the door locked," Geof commented. "It's clear that nobody but you people entered that room while Atheneum McGee was still alive."

He paused to let that sink in.

"What about the other door?" Hardy inquired.

Geof looked blank. "What other door?"

"The one behind the curtain that leads from the choir room directly into the sanctuary. I don't think we ever locked it while we were talking to McGee because nobody was likely to try to come in that way."

"Oh," Geof said. I had the feeling that because he was in a

pastor's study he refrained from saying what he was really thinking. "Terrific. Another door."

But while Hardy's announcement caused him vexation, it produced an audible sigh of relief among the others. Up until the other door came into the picture, our committee offered the only likely suspects. A second door opened, so to speak, the field.

"Well." Geof's shoulders raised in a disgusted shrug. "I'm going to have to ask for your understanding and patience. I'd like to talk to each of you separately before you leave today. Your Honor, why don't we start with you?"

Barbara said bitterly, "There goes the election. I can see the headlines now: MAYOR SUSPECTED IN CHURCH MURDER. Me and my big mouth, Hardy. Why couldn't I just let you have the damn grave?" As she followed Geof out the door, she turned to look back at her fellow committee members. "I would consider it a personal favor," said the mayor to the assembled civic leaders, "if one of you would confess, preferably one of you Democrats."

chapter
15

I was the last to be called into the sanctuary to be questioned. Being last left me alone in the church with Geof and Ailey, all the other committee members having gone home and all the other police officers having finished their distasteful chores. Even Atheneum McGee had departed in more than a spiritual sense: the only remaining trace of him was an outline on the floor where he had fallen, and a surprisingly small spilling of blood.

I sat in Hardy's high-backed chair at the front of the church; Geof's long legs were sprawled out in front of him as he sat beside me in the assistant pastor's chair. Ailey Mason rode the choir rail like a cowboy on a horse.

"Well, this in one for the books," Geof said to Ailey. "What'll we say to his relatives? The good news is your cousin didn't die in Vietnam; the bad news is he didn't live long enough to tell you so."

"What have we got?" Ailey asked rhetorically. "As far as I can tell, Ms. Cain here is the only person who stayed in one place the whole time." His glance at me was no more or less friendly than usual. "At least she says she did."

"You're our ballast, Jenny," Geof said. "You're the only rock in the moving stream of suspects. My God, they're a peripatetic bunch! Not one of them can stand still for more than five minutes at a time. They were in and out of that choir room like flies. To the john. To the drinking fountain. Outdoors for a smoke. Indoors to use the phone. Downstairs for a cup of coffee. Into the john. Back to the choir room. Drop in on you in the study. Meet in the corridor to confer. Back into the choir room. Back to the john." He threw up his hands. "I think they've all got urinary infections."

"That's disgusting," I said, and tried to laugh.

"And the door was always locked," Ailey said.

"Sounds like the title to a murder mystery," I said, "*And the Door Was Always Locked.*"

He ignored me. "The lock was thrown so that every time somebody closed the door, it locked from the inside. That means the killer could have done it anytime he happened to find himself alone in the room with McGee."

"Or," Geof amended, "he might have waited at that side door with the cross, until he heard everyone else leave the room, then gone in and killed him."

"How'd Mary get in that last time," I asked, "if the door was locked and the only person inside was dead?"

"She and her husband have keys to the church," was the simple explanation from Geof. "When she knocked repeatedly and no one came to the door, she opened it herself."

"The way I see it," Ailey hypothesized, "is that the killer could have ingressed either through the front or the side door, but he must have egressed through the side door, then come around the sanctuary to join the rest of the committee in the pastor's study."

"I know who the killer was," I said.

They looked at me expectantly.

"Just look for the bureaucrat among the group," I advised them, "and you'll have your killer. Only bureaucrats ingress and egress; everybody else goes in and out."

Mason flushed, but Geof laughed.

"This seems to support Webster Helms' feelings about sabotage," he said. "Because McGee was killed only *after* he agreed to leave the project and the town out of it and to seek redress from his relatives. And no, Jenny, redress is not something you do when you ingress." He smiled. "But I digress."

"What do you think of Hardy's feelings about a racial motivation?" I wanted to know.

"I think it's an idea," he said neutrally.

"So was the notion that the Earth is flat."

"Yes. Although I am not forgetting about the phone calls you and he received. Maybe they're connected to all this, or maybe they were just the work of a lone crank."

"I suspect all cranks are lone," I said seriously, "even when they're in a group. What other motives do we have?"

"Other motives have we none," Geof sighed.

"So who was alone in the room with him at any time?" I asked.

"Do you really think that anybody is going to tell us that?" Ailey asked sarcastically. "We figure he was probably killed in the last five minutes before your whole committee was gathered back in the study. And during that time . . ."—he pulled out a little notebook, flipped it open and studied it—"Shattuck says he was getting a drink of water in the hall. Sullivan was having a smoke on the front steps. Pete Tower was calling his taco stand. Mary Eberhardt was in the study with you, and her husband had just left there. Jack Fenton was getting a cup of coffee from the canteen in the basement. The mayor was on the phone to her press manager. That little architect was in the men's room. And we know where you say you were."

"And," I added, "Miss Scarlet was in the study with the revolver, Colonel Pickering was in the conservatory with the rope, and someone's in the kitchen with Dinah."

Geof laughed. "That's about it."

"Did anybody have blood on him? Or her?"

"Please." Geof was still chuckling. "If they did, do you think we'd still be here? And no, we didn't find any splinters

95

from the cross stuck under their fingernails." He suddenly sobered, remembering where he was and what he was doing. "We're just funny as hell, aren't we?"

"Geof, while my committee was running hither and yon, where were you and the other cops?"

"Not," he said disgustedly, "outside the side door to the choir room."

"Well, where do you go from here?"

"Home," he said. "Ailey, get something to eat, then find out where McGee was staying while he was here in town. Check with the station to see if they found a motel key on him, and if they found his car. Then go through all his stuff to find the name of a wife we ought to call. It's damn sure his other relatives won't be any help, since they think he's dead." Geof shook his head. "He *is* dead. This is complicated." He tugged at my hand, pulling me to my feet. "Come on, Jenny, let's go home and I'll get a quick sandwich. McGee's not going to be any less dead for my going hungry."

We walked down the center aisle together, each lost in thought. I was musing over how . . . odd . . . the day had been: a stranger appeared out of nowhere, then disappeared into the great beyond. He came, he tried to conquer, he died.

"Odd," I said aloud. Then I realized I was staring straight into the face of Ailey Mason who had preceded us down the aisle.

He looked hurt.

"Not you, Ailey." It being a church, and Sunday, I smiled. He registered surprise, then smiled back.

It was the day's only miracle.

chapter
16

"Do you believe that story Atheneum McGee told?" I asked Geof on the way to his house. "About how he was blown out of a cave in Vietnam and wandered in the jungle? Do you think that really happened?"

"Who knows? We'll check with the army to get their version of what happened to him. We'll see if they think his story could be true."

"It's possible, I suppose."

"It's also possible he went AWOL and he used that story to cover his tracks."

"Yes, but if he lied, he took an incredible chance that the army would catch him. I mean, he couldn't have spent that money in the brig. I wonder if they could have executed him for desertion?"

"Ah-ha," Geof said wryly, "at last, a motive."

He turned into his drive.

"Come to think of it," I said, "we don't know much . . . even if he *was* Atheneum McGee."

"What do you know about him, Jenny?"

"Not much more than you do, I expect. At the time of the

sale of Lobster McGee's property to the developers, there was a question as to whether all the heirs had been properly notified. Atheneum's name came up then. I remember because his name was so odd. And the lawyers had to check carefully to be sure he hadn't left any heirs of his own when he died, supposedly, in Vietnam."

"Did he?"

"I don't remember."

We walked quickly up to his house. Within minutes, we were seated across from one other at the kitchen counter, eating braunschweiger on whole wheat.

"I wonder," I mused aloud, "if the army, or whatever branch of the service it was, actually declared him dead. Or just presumed dead. He made it sound as if a sergeant had identified a body as his and shipped that body home to be buried by the other McGees."

"If he had only been presumed dead," Geof said, "they would have had to wait seven years to have him declared officially kaput."

"Wasn't his great-uncle Lobster declared dead on the basis of a presumption? I mean, they never found his body, did they? But nobody waited seven years to say he was dead. If they had, we wouldn't be building Liberty Harbor now."

"I'm trying to recall." Geof picked up a piece of braun-schweiger that had fallen onto his plate. "Seems to me that was a case in which it was pretty clear as to exactly what had happened. The Coast Guard said he drowned, I don't remember how they knew. But it must have been like what happens when an airplane crashes: they're ninety-nine percent sure they know who was on board, and it's pretty obvious what happened, so they feel safe in declaring that passenger John Doe died in the crash, even if his body was burned to a crisp and blown into the next state."

I put down my sandwich. "Please."

"They must have been equally positive about Lobster," Geof continued imperturbably. "Or maybe they found his body. Maybe it washed up in Freeport." He smiled and swallowed the last bite. "I don't remember. It wasn't a case that landed in a file folder on my desk. Listen, I got my own dead body to worry about, fresh and on view. His great-uncle is no concern of mine."

He removed his plate to the sink, rinsed it and placed it in the dishwasher. I had Wife Number Two to thank for that good training, previous wives not being without their uses to the next woman in a man's life.

The phone rang.

"I'll get it," he said.

"Yeah, Ailey," he said next, then he listened for a few moments. "What do you mean, no car? How'd he get to church? Did you check the cab company? They didn't? No buses out that way on Sunday. He must have walked. Yeah, right, or hitched. So what about the motel?"

Again, he listened.

"Hell," I heard him say, "do we at least know where he came from? All right, hang tight. I'm on my way."

I walked him to the front door.

"Well," Geof said, "he had a wallet on him with an Illinois driver's license in another name, but that's no surprise. If he was hiding from the army, I'd expect that. But he also had an old ID card with his real name on it."

"Atheneum."

"Yes." He patted his pockets for his car keys. "That wallet was all he had on him, Ailey tells me. No car keys, no room key. Hell, maybe he walked all the way from Illinois."

"And slept in the park?"

"He smelled like he slept in the men's room." Geof leaned down to give me a quick but imaginative kiss. I closed the door behind him, kicked off my high heels, and curled up on the living room floor with a pile of Foundation applications.

Denied. Denied. Maybe.

My eyes lifted from an application that put forth a proposal for teaching French and German for travelers to the inmates of our state penitentiaries. I scratched my foot, but it was something in my brain that was itching. I forced my eyes back down to the typewritten application. I wondered which foreign phrases the volunteers would teach the prisoners. "The pen of my aunt is on the table" might not be nearly so useful as "I have a gun. Give me the money and the keys to your car." Denied.

I looked up again, to stare out the window into the front yard. It was brown and dry. *How did Atheneum McGee know that a sergeant had identified another body as his own?*

I dumped the applications off my lap and padded to the phone. Though I had asked for Geof when I was connected with the police station, I had to settle for Ailey Mason.

"Ailey," I said, "where, exactly, in Illinois was Atheneum McGee from?"

"Springfield," he said grudgingly. "Why?"

"Thank you," I said and hung up. I looked up another number in the phonebook and, hesitating only a moment to ask myself if I was sure I knew what I was doing, I dialed it.

"Yes?" a woman's voice replied.

"This is Jennifer Cain." I gave her a second to place me. "I'm the woman who accompanied Detective Bushfield to your house when your husband died."

"Oh, yes."

"Mrs. Reich, I think you ought to know that Atheneum McGee was murdered this afternoon in the Church of the Risen Christ."

I heard her breath taken in sharply.

"He's dead?" And then, for the first time in our short acquaintance, Annie Reich expressed emotion. "Damn him! What about my money!"

chapter
17

Her house had altered in the week since her husband's death, and so had she. At first, we noticed only that the newspapers had piled up on the walk, and no one had hauled the empty trash bins back to the garage from where they leaned against each other on the curb. But then she met us at the door, a different woman.

The once immaculately coiffed hair now hung in lank strands, and when she pushed them carelessly back from her eyes, we saw dark rings under her arms. Those eyes that calmly observed us were still a deep, clear navy, but they evidently no longer saw a need for personal hygiene. Annie Reich had not recently bathed or changed her clothes.

"Come in," she said to Geof, Ailey and me.

We stepped into a room in which Endust had not recently been sprayed. A magazine lay spread in the middle of the floor. There was a half-eaten cheese sandwich on the arm of a sofa and a glass of the omnipresent iced tea tilted precariously against the lower edge of a fireplace. Some of it had spilled, some time ago, leaving a dried, dark pool on the carpet. The house, too, smelled—of things left in a refrigerator too long, of toilets not flushed at once. So, I thought, even she had a time of grief and forgetting, and sympathy began to well within me.

She led us again to the misnamed family room. Again, she brought sweetened iced tea, but the glass that held mine was dirty, and I set it aside. For a strange, suspended moment, we stared at her while she gazed back, placid as a nun, showing no signs of the mild dismay she'd expressed to me over the phone.

"Mrs. Reich," Geof said, finally, "was your husband a sergeant in Atheneum McGee's platoon in Nam?"

"Yes," she said calmly. "How did you find out?"

"At church today," I said, "McGee told a wild story about having been blown out of a cave in Vietnam. He said his sergeant had identified another man's body as his, McGee's that is. I wondered how McGee would have known that, if he was unconscious, as he claimed he was, not to mention having supposedly been blown yards away from the site of the explosion. The only way he could have known that was if he had watched it happen, or if he went AWOL with the help of that sergeant, or he found out about it later.

"I eliminated the first possibility because I didn't think he would have been able to get near enough to know exactly what his sergeant was doing. That left possibilities two or three, both of which seemed to imply that his sergeant knew he was still alive. At that point, I remembered that the only record your husband had was a military one, and that you were from Springfield."

I took a chance on germs and sipped the iced tea.

"This being Massachusetts," I continued, "I thought you meant Springfield, Mass. But of course there are other Springfields, including the one in Illinois. Detective Mason confirmed for me that Atheneum McGee had, indeed, come to Poor Fred from there. So that placed him and your husband in the same city at the same time.

"Then I thought about your presence in church today. Why were you there, I asked myself. I couldn't believe you were a member! And you don't strike me as someone who would go out of her way to witness a spectacle. You sat in the back row. So did McGee. What's more, he arrived at the church without a car. He didn't take a cab. There's no bus service out there on weekends. And the police failed to trace him to a local motel or hotel. So who took him to church this morning? Who put him up for the night?"

She didn't volunteer the answer. Talking to her was like communicating with a slab of uncooked dough. She sat there, large and white and pasty, her chest rising and falling with even breaths. Her eyes were raisins, with the life dried out of them.

"I called you on a hunch," I admitted, "but if it had been a horse race I would have put down money to win. You took him to church today, didn't you? He stayed here in this house with you, didn't he?"

She nodded that massive head, smirking a little.

Suddenly, she burst into speech. "Ansen told me that Atheneum and another man were caught behind the lines by ground fire. They holed up in a cave, just like he said, but it was only for a night before the platoon came back to get them. Anyway, the morning before the platoon came back, the other man stepped out of the cave to look around, and he stepped on a mine. Ansen said it blew his face off. When Atheneum saw what happened, he saw his chance to escape from duty. There wasn't much left on the body to identify it as anybody human, so Atheneum threw down some things that would identify the body as his. Like they'd been blown off him, you know. So when Ansen came back through with the rest of his men, looking for them, he only found the one body. He said they were in a hurry, they were being shot at, I think he called it 'strafed,' and they couldn't stop and check dental records." She smiled briefly, but the joke was hers alone to enjoy. She made it worse by adding, "as if there were any teeth left to check. Anyways, Ansen thought it was McGee. Why shouldn't he of thought that? And he thought the other soldier had been taken prisoner. That's what he reported when he got back to base, and he believed it at the time."

She shifted in her chair, as if moving into another gear. It must have been from park to first, because it sure wasn't overdrive.

"Then a couple of years ago, after Ansen had been back from Vietnam for years, and we were living in Springfield, he ran into McGee again. Knew who he was right away. Atheneum tried to pretend it was all a mistake, that he'd been taken prisoner, and only barely managed to escape with his life. But Ansen figured it out, and McGee finally admitted the truth and begged him not to turn him in to the army." She shrugged. "Ansen wouldn't have done that anyway. What did he care? Why would he do that?"

I said, "So then your husband took the job here, at Liberty Harbor. And when he got here, he heard the story about how the property used to belong to a man named Lobster McGee."

"Yes." She wet her lips. "It was easy after that. I mean, Ansen knew McGee's family was from around these parts, so he figured Atheneum might be a relative of the old guy. So he went back to Springfield and looked him up and told him about his great-uncle's death. And the estate. Ansen said he'd back Atheneum's story about Vietnam if Atheneum would give us a percent of his inheritance."

Geof stirred to life on the couch. "So when your husband died, you took up the cause, is that right, Mrs. Reich?" His voice was blank, devoid of judgment.

"Of course," she said, and a look of vexation crossed her broad features. Both men had failed her, and she was annoyed. I was trying to hold on to my sympathy for her, but it was a losing battle.

I snapped my fingers. "That's what he meant, Geof! When Reich came to my office, he talked about some power I couldn't fight! I thought he was threatening to vandalize the project, but it wasn't that at all. He was talking about the power that Atheneum McGee had, as a rightful heir, to halt the construction of the project!" But then I turned back to her. "Why did he bother with that charade, Mrs. Reich? Why did he pretend to threaten us because of the death of your son?"

She sighed, as at a boy's antics. "Ansen said we were

going to have to live here, and he had to keep his job until Atheneum's inheritance came through. Ansen didn't want people to think we were after the money because of greed. So when Philly died, he saw a chance to make it look as if he was a grief-stricken father who was acting out of revenge. He thought people would be sympathetic to us, that he could keep his job that way."

"But Mrs. Reich," I said, "if Atheneum had brought an injunction to halt the work, your husband would have been out of a job anyway."

"Oh no. My husband just wanted Atheneum to sue his relatives. It was my idea to sue the town and everybody else we could. Ansen was already dead, you see." That smirk of a smile appeared again. "He couldn't lose his job, could he? He was such a fool, Ansen was, caring about appearances the way he did."

Ailey Mason, who had been silent up until then, looked insultingly around the dirty room. He had long before set down his glass of iced tea as if he didn't want to drink anything she had touched. He said, "You don't care about appearances, do you?"

"They won't buy me a condominium in Florida," she said tartly, then faced Geof. "I earned a share of that money. It's still mine. I want it."

Geof stood to go. Looking straight into her blue raisin eyes, he said quietly, "You don't have anything coming to you, and if you did you'd have to climb over me to get it. If I could find charges worth bringing against you, I'd do it, but it's not worth the time and expense. You haven't asked a single question about McGee's murder. Aren't you interested at all?"

She stared dully back at him, resentment pinching the doughy face. "What good does he do me dead? What good do any of them do me dead?"

We left her there, in her own mess.

chapter
18

Instead of returning to the police station, Geof invited Ailey home with us. We fixed strong coffee, then retired to the redwood deck that was attached to the back of the house. It was too muggy to enjoy being outside, but it beat sitting on the floor in the living room. Wife Number Two, Melissa, had taken her furniture with her. Geof, expecting to sell faster than his realtor could manage, never replaced it. There were two kitchen stools, enough furniture for one bedroom and a few patio chairs.

Ailey, Geof and I chose the latter. We had to talk quietly. It was one of those subdivisions in which large houses are jammed as close together as apartments and in which trees are considered natural enemies to that friend of civilization, the bulldozer.

"The course to take now," Geof told us, "is to concentrate on the points of connection between McGee and Reich. They were members of the same platoon in Nam." He ticked the points off on his fingers. "They were connected, whether purposely or not, by Reich's scheme for going AWOL. Connected by their pursuit of a share of

Lobster's estate; by having lived in Springfield, Illinois; and now by murder. Anything I've missed?"

His investigative subordinates shook their heads.

"All right," he continued. "We should be able to draw lines between all those points of connection and make a picture out of it. Now"—he shifted in the webbed chair—"what about the fire at the harbor, and the vandalism of Goose Shattuck's property? What about the charges of racism, and Webster Helms' idea that somebody is trying to prevent the construction of Liberty Harbor? Are those connections we should include in our picture?"

Mason leaned forward and spoke carefully. "You always tell me to keep my eye on the ball. And it looks like the ball we need to watch is murder. Not arson, not vandalism. They might be connected to the murders, but they might not. I think I'd keep my eye on those points you listed, the ones between the two men who were killed." He looked up quickly, then back down at the redwood floor.

"It would be different," I contributed, "if it were only the members of my committee who might have killed Atheneum. That would seem to connect the whole thing irrefutably to Liberty Harbor. But that second door opens to . . . practically anybody."

"It's important to keep in mind," Geof said, "that Reich's murder may have been an accident. At least in the sense that the person who tampered with his brakes had no way of knowing for sure it would kill him."

Mason snorted. "You can't say the same about McGee's death."

We had not turned on the deck lights, but in the darkness I could sense Geof's smile. "No. It's unlikely that somebody tripped into McGee's back with that cross."

"The cross was in the sanctuary, right?" asked Mason.

"Propped against the pulpit," Geof replied.

"Against the *back* of the pulpit," I reminded him. "When Barbara got up to speak, she moved it there, remember? So it was kind of out of sight. I guess somebody came in, picked it up, then walked into the choir room. How many ways are there into the sanctuary?"

"How many petals in a peony?" Geof said gloomily. The figure of speech was so unlikely for the man that Mason and I exchanged glances and laughed. Again, I sensed Geof's smile in the shadows. He said, "One double door to the center aisle, two side doors to the side aisles, the choir room door, a backdoor for the organist, a side door on the west wall for latecomers to the service, and for all I know a trapdoor under the pulpit and a stairway to heaven in the roof."

"There's another possibility," I said slowly, having just thought of it. "We're assuming the murderer came into the sanctuary from outside, picked up the cross, then entered the choir room. Isn't it also possible that he went into the sanctuary *from* the choir room and then returned to it?"

"Yes," Geof said, "it is."

"Can I have some more coffee?" Ailey inquired.

"Help yourself," I suggested, and he got up from his chair to do that. "Why don't you bring the pot back with you, Ailey, and we'll plug it in out here?"

When he was gone from the deck, Geof said softly, "I'll have to go back to the station tonight."

"I know."

"It's been a long time, Jenny."

"I know that, too."

"Somehow," he said, "it seems morally indefensible that murder should take precedence over making love to the one I love."

"There's your motive." I got up and walked over to him in the darkness. "Somebody wants to keep us apart." I leaned down to kiss the top of his head, then his forehead, then the bridge of his nose, the space between his nose and his upper lip, one cheek, the other cheek, the point of his chin . . .

He grabbed my face in both of his hands and placed my lips, finally, on his. "Tease," he whispered. "You're such a tease." He pulled me down on his lap. My back pressed uncomfortably against the metal armrests of the patio chair. "Don't tease me about love and marriage, Jenny."

"I wouldn't do that."

"Make up your mind, please. We've had our experiment in living together without benefit of matrimony. And it's been fun, all right, but so are amusement parks and I wouldn't want to live in one. Even this place . . ."—his arm swept the deck—"it's just a halfway house between my last wife and you."

"I thought we weren't going to talk about this yet."

"How can I buy furniture until I know if you're going to sit in it, too? I want to go shopping for furniture, for God's sake, with you! I want to get the hell out of this temporary shelter for the inadvertently single and . . ."

"My state of singleness is not entirely inadvertent, Geof. Neither, I think you would admit, is yours."

"Don't interrupt me when I'm twisting the facts to my own purpose." He kissed a curve of my neck, sending goosebumps down to my groin. "I want a third chance at marriage, Jenny. Just think how you'll benefit from all the experience I've gained with the first two wives. I made my mistakes with them, and God knows they corrected a multitude of my faults. You can have me as I am now . . . perfect."

I giggled.

"Kiss me there again, please," I requested.

He did, murmuring into my clavicle, "I want to move out of this house and into a house of our own."

"Ted's your realtor," I said gently. "You'd better talk to him about that. It's not my indecision that keeps this house on the market."

"Come on, Jenny." Suddenly he was impatient. "We can afford to support two houses if we have to; hell! at one time I was paying the mortgage on this one, and part of the rent for both Melissa and Roberta."

"Oh Geof, that's the most depressing thing you've ever said. If I were your sister instead of your lover, and I told you I wanted to marry a man who was twice divorced, what would you say to me?"

"Talk about depressing," he said, and slumped back in the chair. His grip on me loosened, as if the tension had evaporated from his muscles.

His beeper broke the silence.

I jumped off his lap so he could get to the damned thing.

"Ailey," he called. The young detective came through the back door with the coffee pot in one hand and his own mug in the other. "Call the station, will you, Ailey? See what they want from me."

Mason wheeled again, taking pot and mug with him.

I reclaimed my chair.

We sat in the darkness waiting for Ailey. It was not a particularly companionable silence.

"Geof." Ailey had forgotten to lower his voice. "They've got him! Those damned vigilantes have caught somebody vandalizing the harbor! It might be our man."

Geof rose quickly and made for the door.

"Uh." Mason blocked his way into the lighted kitchen. "We have to take her."

"Me?"

"Jenny?"

"Yeah." Even in the dim light from the kitchen I could see the suspicion in Mason's eyes. "The suspect says he won't talk to anybody until he sees Jennifer Cain."

chapter 19

"He rowed up to the dock in that little boat."

The pretty young policewoman pointed to a Boston whaler that bobbed in the bay, tied to one of the new docks by lines aft and stern. It was identical to every other one of those beloved, sturdy boats; in fact, it struck me as obscene for that symbol of childhood adventure to have been used to commit an adult criminal act. I hung self-consciously back, feeling inexplicably guilty as if the suspect's insistence on seeing me had linked me to his crime.

The policewoman was an inch or two shorter than I, but broader, stronger, with a tough-looking body that belied the pleasant sweetness of her round face. Her unlikely name was Ashley Meredith.

"They caught him sneaking around the construction site," she was saying to Geof and Ailey. She uttered a short, sharp laugh. "Those damn fool vigilantes damn near killed the son-of-a-gun. The guy who caught him pulled out a gun and fired twice in the air to alert his vigilante pals. You won't believe this. One bullet hit a steel beam. It ricocheted off that. Hit a loose wood plank. Plank fell down and clobbered the suspect. Knocked him cold on his ass."

"Keystone Kops," Ailey muttered.

"Well-intentioned citizens," Geof echoed, "will be the death of themselves. Was the gun registered, Officer Meredith?"

"Yes," she said disgustedly. "So next these guys, they slap him awake again, they tie him up with bunge cord . . ."

"How," Geof interrupted, "in God's name do you do that?"

"I guess it all depends on where you put the hooks," she said, and grinned. "Anyway, they put him in the contractor's office over there. And then they finally got around to calling us. Twenty minutes after the fact, mind you. I'll tell you, sir, they're so damn smug it makes you want to punch 'em out."

"Please," advised Geof, "don't."

We started moving in the direction of Goose Shattuck's office, which was really only a battered trailer that had seen many construction sites in its day. The lights had been turned on inside it. A man's head and torso were silhouetted against a window. His chest looked immense, out of proportion to the sleek head which suggested baldness and which he held stiffly upright as if in defiance or pride. In silhouette, he was unfamiliar to me. How did he know me? Had he seen my name in the local newspaper? Was this the one who had called, spouting racial and sexual filth? Or had he heard of my association with the project? Picked me at random out of a phonebook? I seemed to be attracting the crazies, starting with Ansen Reich. And now this bald, proud felon.

"Who caught him?" Ailey Mason was saying.

I expected Officer Meredith to mention Webster Helms or even Pete Tower, but she named two strangers, a pair of Webster's recruits. His Citizens' Watch Committee had become a popular cause, with so much riding on this project; no doubt they'd been galvanized afresh by the murder of Atheneum McGee. Reluctantly, I gave them credit for accomplishing what the police had not been able to do. Even if this suspect was not the murderer of Ansen Reich and Atheneum McGee, his capture would put an end to the troublesome vandalism. I then wondered why I tended to think of the murderer as one and the same person, rather than two people with, perhaps, separate motives.

We crunched over sand and gravel, the policewoman leading the way, I bringing up the rear.

"When I got here," she said, "I read him his rights, you know, and asked him to identify himself. You'd have thought some peasant had asked the Queen of England for a light! He clammed up like a . . . clam. Acted like I was the damn criminal. Wouldn't say if he wanted a lawyer, wouldn't give a name, didn't have a piece of ID on him. Well, I mean, you'll see why . . . he's wearing a wet suit, and there ain't much room for a wallet. He just kept saying he wanted to see this lady." She jerked her thumb over her shoulder at me. She would have had to be deaf and blind not to have heard the gossip at the station about Geof and me; this escapade would surely feed fresh grist to the rumor mill.

Our hike was lighted by floods that Goose had installed to discourage troublemakers. It was hard to imagine how anyone could manage to hide in all the glare. I said as much to Ashley Meredith.

She barked with laughter again. "I think he thinks he's invisible," she said, and her brown curls shook under her regulation cap. "I'll tell you one thing, if there's one thing this guy is it's visible." There was a surprising undercurrent of admiration in her voice; maybe the intruder was another giant of a man, like Reich?

"What was he up to this time?" Geof wanted to know.

We watched her shoulders rise and fall. "Had a wrench in one hand, they tell me, and a fishing knife in the other. What does that tell you?"

"That maybe we've got our murderer after all," Geof said, a more intense and grim edge to his voice. I wasn't crazy about entering a small room that contained a violent stranger who knew my name. I felt an overwhelming urge to grab Geof's hand and walk away from there, but sternly restrained myself. It did seem to me, however, that civic duty ought to have its limits.

The light that rimmed the closed door of the trailer gave it a false air of welcome. When Ashley Meredith flung open the door, the first person I saw was a short, fat man who was smiling smugly. Definitely one of Webster's. He didn't speak, but waved his arm grandly toward the far end of the trailer as if introducing the main act at the circus. Just in front of me, Ailey Mason made a strange, strangled sound in his throat.

Officer Meredith stood back to let the three of us enter. Before I got both feet in the door, I heard Geof say to someone, "All right, we've brought her."

I stepped in, glanced past the short fat man and his nondescript buddy. Suddenly I was looking full in the face of the man who would not talk to the police until he talked first to me. He was, indeed, wearing a wet suit, complete with a tight black hood that compressed his hair to his scalp, accounting for the bald silhouette. An orange life preserver was fatly fastened around his chest, so that his upper torso seemed disproportionate to the rest of his long graceful body. He was more tanned than you'd expect a man of nocturnal habits to be. His eyes were a fine, clear gray. And the reason for the young policewoman's admiration was apparent: this man, with an edge of silver hair showing at the rim of his black hood, was handsome enough to be famous.

He smiled sweetly at me.

"Geof," I said wearily for the second time that week, "I don't believe you've met my father."

"Mr. Cain," Geof said, more gently than the man deserved. "Did they hurt you? How's your head? Do you want us to call an ambulance?"

"Hold on there!" the short fat man expostulated, but Geof turned a ferocious face on him and waved him to silence. My father, as usual, bypassed the direct questions in favor of ones that had not been asked. "Every night, you know, I watch this project through my binoculars." He nodded wisely at Geof, one guardian of the peace to another. "Just as I promised Jack Fenton I would, you see. Well, this night I saw so many bright lights come on over here. Then as I watched, I saw figures of men moving surreptitiously. I knew I must take action at once. There was no choice but to come ashore and take matters into my own hands." He looked down at the long fingers that had rarely done anything more physical than swing a club or a racket.

Geof looked quizzically at me.

"Ailey," he directed, "get an ambulance over here. I think Mr. Cain may be suffering from concussion."

"Geof," I said, "I wouldn't worry. He's always like this." But when my father raised one of those slender hands to rub the back of his head, I was glad for Geof's concern. I turned to rebuke Web's vigilantes, but they saw it coming and the short fat one stepped forward aggressively.

"How were we to know he was your father?" he demanded, shoving his face into mine. "And what the hell difference does it make? Everybody's somebody's father. Jack the Ripper probably had kids, you know what I mean? This guy here was sneaking around the project up to no good. What was he doing with a knife, you want to tell me that? How about that wrench? Sure, he's your dad, you're going to believe what he tells you, but me, I'm an objective observer, and I say we got our man." He pointed at the dignified figure in the black wet suit. "Right there, by God!"

"Back off," Geof snarled. "Sit the fuck down."

Reluctantly, the short fat one did as he was told, falling heavily back into one of the kitchen chairs that Goose used to conduct business. Behind him, I noticed that the other vigilante had his back turned to us because he was on the phone. With my eyes, I signaled that message to Geof, who prodded Ailey into movement. With two long strides, the young detective had one hand on the man's shoulder and the phone receiver in his other hand. "Say good-bye," said

Ailey gently and handed the phone back to the man, who did as he was told. Ailey then dialed 911 to command an ambulance.

I began to unfasten my father's life preserver. He let me do it for him, much as he would have allowed a valet to undo the diamond studs on one of his tuxedo shirts. "Let's get this thing off, Dad," I said. "You look like you're wearing a beer barrel. Where'd you get the wet suit?"

"Jennifer," he whispered. His eyes twinkled at me. "It was *fun.*"

"Oh Dad." I helped him pull off the black hood. The great mane of silver hair gleamed under the overhead light. "You might have been killed."

I slipped the preserver off his arms, then laid it on the floor of the trailer. It was still damp enough to ring Goose's linoleum with moisture. When I straightened up, I said, "Dad, this is a friend of mine. Detective Geoffrey Bushfield of the Port Frederick police department. And Detective Ailey Mason."

For once, my father's eyes were sharp and attentive.

"Not," he said eagerly, "the Bushware, Inc., Bushfields by any chance?"

"Yes, sir." Geof smiled. "I'm the wayward son."

But my dad was off in other circles, social ones. "Fine parties they used to give, your people. Only the finest wines, the best orchestras. I remember one time for the twenty-fifth anniversary of the company, your mother had the club put out little tool boxes for party favors. Cutest darn thing I ever saw! Why do you know, the wrench I brought over here with me is a Bushware wrench!" He looked around for it, finally sighted it on the kitchen table which served as Goose's desk, and pointed proudly at it. Then, mercurial as always, he seemed to droop in his wet suit. "We lost something in this godforsaken burg when your family moved away." His face was as long and sad as Gatsby's ever was when he mooned over Daisy. "Nobody can play as good a game of doubles at the net as your father could. Does he still play?"

"Tennis?" Geof looked bemused. Ailey stared at my father as if he were a strange creature from another star.

"Yes, sir, I think he still plays. Mr. Cain, when did you get back to town?"

"Geof!" I said, not believing what I heard.

"I'm sorry," he said, turning to me with real regret on his face. "But you know I have to go through the formalities, your father or not. Just bear with me, all right?"

"Yes, all right." But suddenly I was nervous, a state that was not improved when Webster Helms flung open the trailer door with a startling bang.

"Congratulations!" he said loudly to his vigilantes, who had brightened considerably at his entrance. Now I knew whom they'd called so quietly: their Great White Leader. Webster wheeled on my father like vengeance personified. "Jimmy Cain!" he said, puffing out his thin chest. "It wasn't enough that you singlehandedly threw this town into a recession by putting hundreds of people out of work! No! You had to come back to destroy our renaissance!"

"Webster!" I was frightened by the expression on my father's face. He seemed, for once, to be listening to the person who was talking to him. And suddenly I was afraid that my father was going to get hit by the realization of his shortcomings right there in that tatty trailer surrounded by people who didn't love him or know him. He looked as if he had been struck by a blow that was infinitely more painful than any that a loose board could inflict.

Geof had opened his mouth to stop Webster, but the little architect would not be halted. He whirled on the detectives and shouted, "I want this man in jail where he belongs! Everybody knows that Jennifer is your lover, Bushfield, and you'd better not show any preferential treatment of this . . . criminal . . . or the whole town will want to know why!"

"Stop it, Web," I pleaded. "Please, can't you see what you're doing to . . ."

"*You* look at him, Jennifer," Webster said, more calmly. "What you see is a man who hasn't been back to this town in years, am I right? And he just happens to come back when all this trouble starts, am I right? And he just happens to be apprehended on the site of the project which has just happened to be the site of acts of violence and sabotage, am

I right? I'm saying that he ruined this town once, and he means to do it again."

I felt as if I couldn't breathe, as if the walls of the trailer were sliding in on me and my family, squeezing out of us what little was left of the juice and flavor of life. This couldn't be happening, not again. I thought of my mother who still hovered, comatose and certifiably crazy, in a mental institution; of my sister who was only beginning to come out from under the shame of my father's earlier failure; of Geof, who had not bargained on this public disaster when he dreamed his wedding plans for us.

Somebody said, "Jennifer," in a gentle, loving voice.

But I was lost in the confused, hurt gray eyes of my father. "Jenny," he said, "does this mean they won't name the harbor after us?"

chapter
20

"Jenny." Geof spoke privately to me a few minutes later when we were outside again under the floodlights. It was going on eleven o'clock. "Of course I'll let him go. I have no intention of allowing him to go to jail. But you understand that he was trespassing on plainly marked private property, and that it will be worse for him in the long run if I don't put him through the usual drill. Because he's your father, I'll have to be extremely careful to see that he receives no preferential treatment." He smiled slightly. "At least no overt preferential treatment."

My father sat in the back of an ambulance, staring out the window at me like a puppy in a pet shop.

"I can't bear this," I said.

"Sure you can. Listen to me. This all depends on whether or not the owners of the mall decide to press charges. And since I'm the one who's going to describe tonight's events to them, you can be fairly sure they won't do it."

"I don't want you to get into trouble." In truth, I might have sacrificed anything or anybody to avoid this latest family humiliation.

119

He smiled. "I've been known to take care of myself. You want to come down to the hospital and then to the station with us, don't you?"

"Yes. And no."

"That's what I thought." He gave me the keys to his car. "Follow us then. And don't worry any more than you absolutely have to, do you hear me? I'll take care of your father. He is a funny old guy, isn't he?"

"How nice of you to put that interpretation on it. Oh God, wait until the papers get wind of this. Wait until my sister hears about it. Lord, I guess I'd better call my stepmother in California. And our lawyers. And . . ."

"Don't," he said sternly. "Don't break down now, I mean. He needs you."

"You haven't any idea of the irony of that statement."

"I know all about that, Jenny," he said. "I know how little he was there when you needed him. At the moment, that's irrelevant, don't you think? He's your father. You're his only functioning daughter. Sometimes life comes down to equations as simple and basic as that."

"You have an overdeveloped sense of duty." But I reached up to kiss him on the cheek. The hell with Webster Helms and Officer Ashley Meredith and all the others who were avidly watching us with sidelong glances. If there was anything I'd learned from my crazy family, it was if you're going to make a spectacle of yourself, by God make a *spectacle* of yourself.

Then I followed my father to the hospital.

Four hours later, he was released into my custody. I couldn't take him to stay at Geof's house with me, because of the uproar that would cause—SUSPECT ROOMS WITH TOP COP—so Geof drove us over there, I packed a few of my things, put my exhausted father into my car and moved onto the *Amy Denise* with him.

He was staying in the large aft cabin where Geof and I had unsuccessfully tried to spend one night. I moved myself into the forward V-berth. My father went quietly to bed without inquiring what I intended to do with him next. What I did was to climb to the bridge, start the engines and steer us to an out-of-the-way cove that I knew. I dropped anchor in the middle of it, out of shouting reach of the shore. Any reporter who wanted this story would have to find us first and then row through heavy chop to reach us. It was uncomfortably bumpy for us in that cove, too, but that was a small price to pay for refuge, no matter how temporary or illusory.

When I crawled into my narrow bunk it was five o'clock in the morning of another hot and cloudless day. There were, however, clouds on my internal horizon. They didn't keep me from sleeping.

My travel alarm clock went off at seven. Work awaited, regardless of the fate of feckless and/or felonious fathers. The night before, in order to get to the *Amy Denise* anchored in Liberty Harbor Bay, we had had to take the Boston whaler back out again. Because the Citizens' Watch Committee was convinced it had its man, they'd gone home, so there was no one to stop us. Geof had managed to delay the impounding of the Boston whaler for evidence, a sleight of hand he'd have to deal with when he faced his higher-ups in the morning. I had the queasy feeling I was corrupting an honest cop, one who might decide that the price of having me was not worth the loss of his integrity. But on this morning, I was practically, not philosophically, minded.

Rather than go to the considerable effort of winching the small boat up to the bridge of the *Amy Denise,* I had merely tied her to the aft deck and crossed my fingers. Now she was still there, bobbing happily in that way that Boston whalers have of seeming to say, "Let's play." I rolled up my business clothes in a plastic trashbag, then stuck my purse and briefcase in it as well, left my father a stern note on the refrigerator, and climbed down the swim ladder to the little boat. I was commuting to shore in a swimming suit. The whaler had an engine which my father the spy had chosen not to use the night before, opting, instead, for the stealthy silence of the oars; for once in my life, I followed his lead.

No use advertising our comings and goings with any more noise than necessary. I rowed to shore, knowing a short walk would take me to a pay phone, which would get me a taxi, which would take me back to the marina so I could pick up my car and go to the office.

By ten, I was dry, dressed and walking in the door to be greeted by Faye Basil and Derek Jones.

"Just because you're the boss," my assistant said grumpily, "doesn't mean you get to sleep 'til noon!"

chapter
21

Within the hour, it was clear that my presence was not only *not* a help to the Port Frederick Civic Foundation, but that it was a hindrance of awesome proportions. As if through some intuitive cue, the deluge of phone calls began as soon as I sat down at my desk and tried to focus on the work for which I was being paid.

My sister Sherry got to me first, the press having gotten to her first. She was strangely, uncharacteristically calm. "I don't have anything to do with this," she informed me in clipped tones. "I don't have anything to do with him. I am leaving town. I am packing and going away to Europe on the next Concorde and I am taking my family with me. I am not hysterical, Jenny. Please note that I am not hysterical. I am merely leaving, that's all. If they hang him, save me a piece of rope for old times' sake." Now that was more like the loving sister I knew so well.

"Bon voyage," I said without bitterness. Any crisis was easier to handle with her out of the way. As for my ailing mother, there was no reaching her with this or any other

news. It was going to be Dad and me, alone together on the deep blue sea.

Her call was followed in quick and frantic order by one each from two local newspapers, a TV station, three radio stations, the regional cable affiliate and a reporter from Boston who'd already got wind of the news. To each in turn I said politely, "No comment."

"What's your dad got against that town?" the reporter from Boston pressed. I was just tired enough to be goaded into answering her.

"This is his home," I replied. "He loves it like any other native son."

"Is this part of a conspiracy that includes the bankruptcy of Cain Clams?" she asked sharply.

"Oh, please," I said in disgust.

"Have they charged him yet with the murders of that man Reich and that what's-his-name McGee fellow?"

"No! And there is no reason for you to assume they will. My father had nothing to do with those tragedies. Please don't jump to such awful conclusions."

"I hear he was a champion archer at Dartmouth."

"Oh, Lord," I sighed. "He went to Brown for half a semester in his freshman year before he flunked out. To my knowledge he has never lifted a bow and arrow in his life."

"But he's a mean man with a wrench," she said nastily.

I hung up on her, something I should have done several questions earlier. But she was the only ugly one among the dozen or so who called; the others were locals who knew me personally. They were courteous, apologetic, as kind as they could be considering the questions they had to ask. "It's a terrible sign," I said to Faye, "when reporters are kind and gentle with you. It means they like you, and they sure are sorry, but they're going to crucify you because they think you're guilty as hell. They think he did it, Faye."

She reached across my desk to pat my hand.

I felt my eyes fill and quickly blinked.

"Your father," she said sweetly, "wouldn't kill a fly. Mainly because it would never occur to him to do it himself."

I looked up at her in surprise, saw the kind twinkle in her eyes and began to laugh. I was still smiling, and feeling cheered, when the phone began its siren call again.

"Jennifer," said Webster Helms with a new formality in his voice that boded ill for my family. "I was appalled to learn this morning that your father has been released instead of being held in jail where he should be. I am sorry, Jennifer, but the man is a menace to this community. I think it only fair to warn you that I intend to do everything in my power to see that the full force of the law is brought to bear against him and that a full-scale investigation of his recent activities be launched by an independent, nonbiased investigator."

"Are you reading that, Webster?" I said recklessly. "Or did you memorize it before you called?"

There was a moment of charged and angry silence on both ends of the line. Finally he said stiffly, "Don't say I didn't warn you, Jennifer."

I let him hang up first.

Immediately, the phone buzzed again. I let it ring. I looked into the outer office where my staff was pretending to work on grants, investments and applications. Then I punched another outside line, first to let Ted Sullivan know where I'd taken his boat, then to call the First City Bank.

"Jack Fenton, please," I said to the switchboard.

His secretary put me through immediately, her voice so tactfully devoid of expression that it told me hundreds of things I didn't want to hear about how the average citizen was reacting to the news of my father's arrest and release.

"I'm so sorry," Jack said as soon as he came on the line. "What can I do to help you, Jennifer?"

"He didn't do it, Jack. He didn't do anything but play James Bond for a night."

"I know that, my dear."

"Oh," I said, and leaned my forehead into my open palm. "Thank you for that. I'll tell you what else you can do for me if you would: you can assume the authority for giving me an early vacation, and clear it later with the rest of the board."

He clucked sympathetically. "Yes, it's probably hell trying to work through all this."

"It's not that," I said. "Well, yes, it is hell. And as long as this continues, and as long as I continue to hang around the office, this Foundation will suffer from lack of work and concentration. But that's not the only reason I want the time off, Jack." I was beginning to feel clear-headed for the first time that morning. "My father didn't do any of the things people are assuming he did. You and I both know that as well as we know there's no Santa Claus. But somebody did it, Jack. Somebody killed Reich. Somebody killed McGee. Somebody shot those burning arrows into Webster's shack and somebody got to Shattuck's vehicles. Maybe it's one and the same person, maybe it's not. But finding out who it is may be the only way I'll ever clear my father in the mind and heart of this city."

"Jennifer, the police . . ."

"Are having a tough enough time as it is," I said bluntly, "because of the conflict of interest charges that are arising out of my relationship with Geof Bushfield."

"A crusade is a lonely and dangerous undertaking," he said slowly. "Sometimes crusaders don't come home at all. And sometimes they find their holy grail is made of brass, and tarnished."

I laughed softly. "My father would be so insulted, Jack, to think you considered him anything less than twenty-four-karat gold."

The old banker chuckled, and I knew I'd won. "All right," he said, giving me the feeling I'd just passed muster for a loan, "you do what you have to do. I'll clear the road for you with the other trustees."

"Thank you."

"You be careful, young lady."

"I will. Bless you."

Next, I called the police station with every intention of informing Geof about what it was I intended to do. I was even going to ask his advice and enlist his aid in my quest.

"I'm taking a few days off," I said, "until this thing gets straightened out or blows over." And then I opened my mouth to tell him the rest of it. And couldn't do it. At any rate, didn't do it. "Geof," I should have said, "I'm going to launch a little private investigation of my own to try to clear my father. Yes, I know it sounds like another vigilante committee—a group of one, in this case—but I'm more personally involved than Web and his cohort. There's not much left to my family name in the way of honor, but I'll be damned if I'll let them besmirch it falsely. I have to do this in the same way that I have to eat and sleep."

That's what I should have, might have, didn't say.

Instead, I added lamely, "I'd better stay close to my dad to keep him out of trouble."

"I agree," Geof said, so understandingly he doubled my guilt factor to an eight point five on a ten-point scale. "You know, this may not be what you want to hear, but I kind of liked him, Jenny. It's not as if he *wants* to be a failure as a father or a husband. Or a businessman. I mean, the crazy irresponsible things he does only make it appear that way. The truth is, he wants approval and success as much as anybody. If there ever was a man whose actions belie the true motives of his heart, it's your dad."

"I don't think," I said evenly, "that an acquaintance of a few hours gives you lecturing privileges. May I respectfully point out that you haven't known him as long or as well as I have."

"You may," he said quickly, apologetically. "And God knows you should. Listen, keep in regular touch with me, all right? I promise not to preach, and I'll keep you informed about what's going on with our various and multitudinous investigations." He sighed wearily, having not had much more sleep than I. My guilt factor rose to an even nine points.

But if I were to make an ass of myself, it seemed better, kinder, to do it alone. Better to do my searching and probing and questioning without burdening him with the need to give me an official "No," or an unofficial "Okay, but I wish you wouldn't." Life was complicated enough for him now, with his connection to the Calamity Cains; better to leave him out of my activities as much as possible.

That was the good news part of my rationale; the bad news part was that the night's crises had left me feeling allied with my father in an us-against-the-world sort of way, that world unfortunately including policemen. Maybe it was only the effect of exhaustion, but I felt separated from Geof by a fog of suspicion, accusation, conflict of interest and doubt.

"Jenny," he was saying, "there's one thing I want you to remember while you're lying out there in the sun on that boat."

"What's that?"

"I love you."

Bingo: ten.

Saying good-bye to him depressed me. But then I put it out of my mind, clicked my briefcase and purse closed, grabbed both of them and walked over to Faye's desk. After a few words of explanation and instruction, I said, "Tell whoever calls that I am on vacation and cannot be reached. I'll call you every day to check on things. But basically it's in your hands, yours and Derek's and Marvin's. Frankly, I think you'll get more done without me."

She looked at me sadly, without arguing the point.

I left the Foundation, wondering if my bosses, the trustees, could any longer afford to keep as director someone whose name was so frequently associated with scandal. "Good-bye," I said, looking back. I felt depressed all over again.

chapter
22

The taxi took me back to Geof's house. With a running meter to encourage speed, I changed into a cool cotton skirt and blouse, then packed sufficient clothes to last, with frequent washings, a couple of weeks. Then the taxi returned me to my car at Liberty Harbor. From there I drove up to the old lover's leap that overlooked the bay.

I was trying to carve a niche of time to think, relax, gain some perspective. A trip to the mountains accomplishes that end for some people, but it's always the sea that refreshes me. I don't have to be on it or in it. I only require a warm rock from which I can watch waves.

After I pulled off the highway, I parked the car and walked over to the edge of the low cliff. I leaned cautiously against the dilapidated wood fence that separated me from a long fall into the filthy lobster pound directly below. I made a mental note to remind the committee to try to prod the city into refurbishing this future tourist attraction. Then I smiled to myself when I recognized the track of familiar routine along which my mind was running: check on this, push for that, meet with them, read it, say it, do it. All of which assumed a life in which routine was made possible by the security of employment, position, relationship. And it was those examples of life's little predictable regularities on which I suddenly had only the most tenuous hold.

I released my hold on the top of the fence, hoping that didn't symbolize anything profound. At a gap in the fence there was a not-very-clean, not-very-grassy verge. I kicked away a few pieces of litter of recent vintage, sat down on the ragged piece of green and pulled a small notebook out of my skirt pocket. Ailey Mason would have approved. Regulation rookie equipment: one blank notebook. I would have preferred to use my home computer, but it was there at Geof's and I was here. Below me, Goose Shattuck's men labored on the mall, unimpeded by death or destruction. Drills roared, hammers fell, saws rasped, trucks rolled along the dirt, men crawled like cautious crabs along the high horizontal beams. Neither murder nor vandalism had stopped, or even slowed down, this renovation we all wanted so badly.

I took a ballpoint pen from my other skirt pocket.

First heading: *Sequence of (Known) Main Events*— Saturday, June 12, Ansen Reich killed. Sunday, June 13, vandalism and arson. Sunday, June 20, Atheneum McGee killed. I did not list my father's foray as a main event.

Second heading: *Subsidiary, possibly pertinent events*— Friday, June 11, Ansen Reich threatens project. Monday, June 14, Citizens' Watch Committee formed; Unmarked Grave approved; Cain and Eberhardt receive racist phone calls. Sunday, June 20, Mrs. Reich reveals scheme to get percentage of Atheneum McGee's inheritance; James Cain apprehended while trespassing at project.

Third heading: *Suggested Motives*—1) Sabotage: A person or persons are trying to harm the project for reasons unknown. 2) Conspiracy: James Cain is trying to harm the project as part of an overall plan to damage Port Frederick. 3) Racism: Somebody is trying to harm the project as a protest against minority involvement.

Fourth heading: *Supporting Data*—1) The idea of a racist

motive is supported by the phone calls to Jenny and Hardy; by the use of the cross of the Unmarked Grave as a murder weapon; by . . .

I quickly ran out of steam on that one. I put down my pencil.

The idea of a conspiracy motive on the part of my father was supported by his sudden appearance in town just at the time of the main events; by his history of causing economic problems for the town, although that was through mismanagement and not through malfeasance; and by his act of trespassing on the project while in possession of potentially deadly weapons.

But the conspiracy motive came smack up against the man himself who couldn't organize a trip to the grocery store, much less a conspiracy. That teakettle wouldn't boil, either.

As for the sabotage . . . what was the actual damage to the project? The foreman died, but he was quickly replaced, so the work continued unabated. The arson destroyed a shack and a pier, but the pier was due for demolition anyway, and the shack was quickly rebuilt, so the work continued unabated. . . .

I frowned and gazed out to sea again, my notes forgotten.

The damage to Goose Shattuck's vehicles was personally aggravating for him, but he probably had them fixed by Monday morning so that he could make it to work on time. And work continued unab—

A sailboat, two-masted, was rounding the bend into the bay. I focused on it until it rounded the first buoy, when my vision blurred with the intensity of my thinking.

As for the death of Atheneum McGee, which was the next main event after Reich's murder and the arson and vandalism, it had no effect on the project at all. He was already thought to be dead, so his share of the estate had already been split among the other heirs. Thus, work at the project continued unabated.

Below me, work continued.

Unabated.

Geof had never seemed to commit himself to an acceptance of the sabotage theory that Web so enthusiastically endorsed from the beginning. Now why was that, I asked myself, why was an experienced cop so loath to grab the nearest handy motive?

I pulled my back up straighter.

Because, I realized, there had only been an appearance of sabotage, but no real damage, nothing to impede the orderly progress of construction. "I'll believe it," Geof had said of the sabotage theory, "when I see specific evidence to prove it."

Something else he'd said to me that morning came unbidden into my head: "Your father doesn't want to fail. The things he does only make it seem that way. His actions belie the true motives of his heart."

Below, work on the project continued.

Unabated.

The events of the past ten days seemed on the surface to suggest a violent antipathy to Liberty Harbor. But the net result was no damage at all, at least not sufficient to stop the work. And that would seem to suggest that someone's actions belied the motives of his heart.

If I was right, the person or persons who were causing the trouble did not intend to harm the project at all! Could I then logically infer the reverse? Did they desperately want it to succeed? And so their acts were somehow intended to further that goal? But how would Ansen Reich's death advance the project? Or Atheneum's murder? How could arson and vandalism be interpreted as positive acts?

Keep your eye on the ball, Geof always told Ailey.

The ball is murder, Ailey had suggested.

If Reich and McGee were murdered to advance the project in some way, the violent acts might only be camouflage to entice the authorities into looking for other motives, ergo other suspects. Arson and vandalism were the spit on that ball that caused it to swerve deceptively toward the batter so he couldn't keep his eye on it.

New heading: *Who Needs Project to Succeed?*—

Ruthlessly, I made my list of familiar names. Then I stood, brushed off the dirt and grass, stuck my pencil and notepad in my pockets and returned to my car.

First I would force down some lunch.

Then I would ask my questions.

chapter
23

The lunch rush was long over by the time I stepped into the cool, shaded welcome of The Buoy. There was nobody out front in the long dim hall that served as a coatroom and lobby, and I heard only a low murmur punctuated by occasional clatters of silver and dishes from within. I thought I'd get a quick sandwich and be gone before the afterwork crowd arrived for their wine coolers and light beers.

But first I slipped into the old-fashioned phone booth in the hall, pulled the folding door shut, flipped down the wooden seat and sat on it, pulled the phonebook on its chain toward me and thumbed to the section with U.S. government phone numbers. I dialed in my credit card number for a long-distance call.

"Federal Reserve Bank," said the switchboard.

I gave the name of an attorney I knew and was channeled through her secretary before I heard the memorable voice, a throbbing contralto that ought to have been thrilling juries in courtrooms instead of bankers in boardrooms.

"Jennifer Cain." She made my name sound like a late-breaking news bulletin. "As I live and breathe. It's not time for our college reunion yet, is it? I'm not that old yet, am I?"

"Sandra," I replied, "the years will never show on that face. Even at our fiftieth reunion, the bartender will demand to see your driver's license before he'll serve you a drink."

"Whatever it is you want," she said dryly, "it's yours. And as I recall, I owe you one from that time you lifted that drunken and rapacious law clerk off my body and heaved him singlehanded out of your date's car onto his bare butt."

"It's gracious of you to recall that," I said, "so that I don't have to crudely remind you. I need information, Sandra. I have some crazy cousins who are thinking of making a try for majority ownership of the First City Bank in this town. It's none of my business, except they want our family's stock, too. I'd like your unofficial, absolutely off-the-record feeling in regard to the general well-being of that bank. Its loan picture, management, reputation, you know."

"Fenton's First? My heavens, it's as old as the Republic and a hell of a lot better managed. Why that bank is a paragon on which every other bank in this state could model itself, and Jack Fenton is a saint among bankers. Why that man makes George Washington look like a liar and Abe Lincoln look like a cheat. To impugn his banking wisdom is to deny God. Worse, it's a communist plot. Jenny," she said suspiciously, "these cousins of yours, are they Democrats?"

"Sandra, the First has out a lot of big loans to various people for a project that we call Liberty Harbor."

"I've heard of it," the Bostonian said condescendingly.

"Well, what do you hear in regard to their loans vis-à-vis their equity? Could they have overextended themselves on this one?"

"Don't," said the throbbing contralto, "be silly."

Before she hung up, she added, "Jenny, my advice to you is to tell your cousins to go fish in another pond. This one is frozen so solid they couldn't break into it with a crowbar."

"I doubt," I said, "that you'll hear any more about them. Thanks, Sandra. Good-bye."

I squeezed out of the phone booth and followed my nose

toward the restaurant which was in an oak-planked room off the bar. "Jenny!" called the bartender, a member of the latest generation of the same family that had owned The Buoy for generations. But when I looked up, I could see flooding into his broad, open face a sudden recollection of the latest scandal involving my father. He flushed for lack of anything to say, then bent his head to apply himself furiously to polishing the brass rail along his bar. I found myself smiling at the top of his head. There was a bald spot there, the size of a silver dollar. I said hello to it, then forced myself to stroll into the restaurant at a pace that implied no cares in the world, but mentally I braced myself for the familiar faces I might find there.

But there were only strangers, except for a corner table where it looked as if a hooker and her pimp were negotiating with a Baptist deacon. It was Betty Tower, in ruffles and pink spike heels, Pete Tower, looking beefy and middle-aged in a black suit, and Webster Helms. They seemed to be arguing about something, and were hunched over their cups of coffee like gnomes over gold. They didn't see me. I walked steadily toward them until they did.

"Jenny!" Betty said brightly. "Look Pete, Web. It's Jenny."

The men looked up at me with large smiles to show how delighted they were to see me. They were so delighted they were speechless. I eased myself down into the empty fourth chair at their table and smiled back at them.

"Hello," I said. "Mind if I join you?"

"Love it! We'd simply love it!"

"Why of course we wouldn't mind, Jenny!"

"Have you ordered? No? Waitress, a menu . . ."

They were all over themselves in their eagerness to display their broadmindedness. While they babbled on to each other about what a lovely day it was and did anyone think it might rain?, I ordered a glass of light ale and a crab sandwich. When the waitress departed, I clasped my hands on the table in front of me, and smiled back at the trio.

"Dad's doing fine," I said as if they'd asked.

"Great!" Pete Tower said, as fervently as if I'd told him he would live forever. "That's just great!"

Webster Helms looked daggers at him. The architect then turned on me his most forthright gaze. "I'm sorry this sad business with your father affects you, Jennifer," he said somberly. "But it's nothing personal, you understand. We have to think of the good of this city."

"Well," I said, "the renovation is important to us all."

He looked surprised at the mildness of my response, and seemed visibly to relax.

"Important," Pete pronounced, "the very word for it. Important, yes."

His wife gave him a look that would steam clams. I turned toward her with my most winning, humble smile. "I guess every one of us has a stake in the project, don't you think, Betty? I mean, the Foundation has invested quite a bit of money in it, at my urging, so it's important . . ."—I smiled in a kindly way at Pete—"to me for it to succeed. I want to look good with my bosses, you know!" I gave a little laugh that I hoped was convincing. "And there you are, the two of you, with that wonderful café about to open. I do hope this business with my father has not delayed your opening in any way?"

"It better not," she snapped, and pushed her coffee away. Under her makeup, the little red veins that splayed out from her nose were blazing. Her husband turned pink above his white collar and stirred his own coffee vigorously. Betty said, "I don't mind telling you that we've got ourselves in hock up to our eyeballs on this, Jenny. It's no secret. If we don't make our balloon payment on time this fall, the bank will have our ass in a sling."

"Now, Betty," her husband remonstrated weakly. "Jenny doesn't want to know our problems."

"I don't see why not," she snapped back. "Her crazy father could have ruined us, same as he ruined all those employees when their plant went belly up." She glared defiantly at me, daring me to deny it. The men shifted uneasily in their chairs.

Instead, I smiled sadly. "And you, Web," I murmured, "an architect in a town this size doesn't get many opportunities of this magnitude. You've probably had to turn down other jobs to get it completed, or did you add more employees?"

"Both," he said grandly. "When one wins a job like this over the bids of competitors from larger metropolitan areas, one wants to do one's best to prove one's worth, you know. For the pride of one's city, you know."

"I know." I nodded slowly. "One does, indeed."

Pete smiled agreeably, as he did to most things Webster said, but his wife eyed me suspiciously. Before she could open her frosted-pink lips, I said, "Goose probably feels as you do, Webster. I mean, this is a grand project on which to retire in full glory. I'll bet its success means as much to him as any job he's ever won."

"More," Betty informed me, then laughed. "He's got to keep those young turks at bay. They've been getting all his jobs because everybody thinks Goose is too old to hack it anymore. Why d'ya think he bid it so low?"

"He's only sixty," I protested.

She shrugged her pink, ruffled shoulders, obviously bored with talk of anyone but herself, and any interests but her own.

"You see, Jennifer," Webster Helms bore down on me as I'd hoped he would, "this renovation is vitally important to any number of us. Just take the members of our committee, for instance." He ticked off names and, unknowingly, motives on his fingers. "Frankly, it will boost my firm's reputation to a national level, it will help us win bids for major developments outside of this state. And you've already heard how important it is to Betty and Pete. Why their whole future is riding on that pretty little café that I've designed for them."

"Well," Pete demurred hesitantly, "we do have one or two other little interests that . . ."

"And Goose," Web rolled implacably on, "well, Betty's right about Goose needing this one to prove he can still cut the mustard. You take the rest of our committee—there isn't one person who won't stand to gain from this business. I mean, Ted Sullivan will sell more houses because more people will be employed . . ."

"More?" Betty laughed explosively. "He should sell one house and be lucky . . ."

". . . and if they're making money they'll be able to move up in the world, to better houses. And the First City Bank will get rich on interest payments, so Jack Fenton will be a happy man."

"He could retire on our interest." Betty's makeup creased between her eyes when she frowned.

". . . Hardy and Mary Eberhardt will cement their position as leaders of the black community because of all those jobs we're giving them . . ."

I bit my tongue viciously and managed to keep smiling through Web's lecture on the trickle-down theory of Economics 101.

". . . and Barbara could probably get reelected solely on the strength of the goodwill this project will generate for her administration once it's completed. And you, Jennifer . . ." Webster smiled, his thin lips almost disappearing into his mouth. "You'll get a raise for being the smart girl who recommended the harbor to your trustees for funding."

Smiling was becoming increasingly more difficult, what with my jaws clenched so tight I thought my teeth would break.

"As if she needed the money," Betty muttered.

"So you see . . ." Web rolled on to his grand finale, spreading his hands wide in candor and fellowship. He had on a short-sleeve shirt and I could see the blue veins on the inside of his forearms. "We're all depending on this project to be completed successfully and right on time." Suddenly his face was pinched. "If that does not happen, it will be the death of this town!"

"Crab?"

We looked as one at the waitress.

"Who's got the crab?" she asked. "And the brew?"

Webster looked nonplussed, his dramatic moment ruined.

I ate quickly, gulped my ale so fast I was dizzy when the glass was empty, and excused myself, content in the knowledge that I was leaving with a fistful of possible motives, all obligingly supplied by some of the suspects.

"Au revoir," I said to Betty and Pete Tower. To the head of the Port Frederick Citizens' Watch Committee, I said, "Heigh-o Silver, away."

I was aware of the silence that reigned behind me as I made my way to the door. At the entrance to the bar, I glanced back: the gnomes were counting their gold again.

On the way out, I passed the mayor coming in.

"Jenny!" She smiled that bright, false smile I had seen on the faces of her three pals and the bartender. I doubled the wattage and gave it right back to her. She said, "I'm so sorry to hear about your father, Jenny. You know I don't believe a word of it, not a word of it, you know that."

"Thank you, Barbara. Perhaps you'll call the judge and put in a good word for my dad?"

"Gosh." She looked at her watch. "Is it that late? I'm so hungry I could eat chicken at a political banquet. Good to see you, Jenny. Keep in touch!"

"I'm not going on vacation, Barbara."

But she was gone, sweeping through the door into the bar.

When I pulled out of the parking lot in my car, I passed Goose Shattuck driving into it in his black Cadillac. I waved, but he didn't see me. I honked, but he didn't turn his head. He was either preoccupied, or purposely avoiding me.

I was beginning to get a feeling for who my friends were, and they weren't gathering at The Buoy that afternoon. "The hell with them," I said aloud to the windshield, and pretended it didn't hurt.

Then I drove to the bank.

chapter
24

"You have a friend at the First," declared the poster in the bank window. I hoped it was true.

"No, I don't have an appointment, Mrs. Alonzo," I admitted to Jack Fenton's white-haired secretary. She tried not to frown at the news. She picked up a ruler from her desk; I hid my knuckles behind my back. Mrs. Alonzo—I'd never heard her first name, even the brass plate on her desk said MRS. ALONZO—sat in lone, regal splendor, like the Queen Mother, at a mahogany desk at the rear of the nineteenth-century building. Behind her, the intricately carved wooden door to Jack's office was pointedly closed to drop-in visitors like me. I smiled winningly, and said, "But I wouldn't ask to see him if it weren't important. Could you get me a few minutes with him?"

She pressed a button on her old-fashioned intercom.

"Mr. Fenton," she said when he answered, "I know how busy you are, and I'm sorry to bother you, but Miss Cain, who does not have an appointment, is here to see you." Those were her words. Her tone said, "Miss Cain, who is in the first infectious stages of a dread disease, is here to see you."

"Jennifer? Here?" crackled the familiar voice. "Send her in! I'm not doing a damn thing. That's the trouble with being good at delegating authority: pretty soon you wind up with nothing at all to do. Send her in, please, Mrs. Alonzo."

Mrs. Alonzo sighed, as must the Queen Mother when one of her grandchildren acts up, and waved me into the chairman's office.

Jack was waiting for me on the other side of the door. He was trim and distinguished in banker's gray with black pinstripes. "A banker," he'd been known to crack, "must never appear in the red." He took my arm and escorted me to a wood and brown leather chair opposite his desk, which was not as massive as Mrs. Alonzo's. Instead of returning to his swivel chair behind the desk, Jack pulled up a chair to sit near me. It looked as if I did indeed have a friend at the First, although if he'd known that I was checking up on him, with an eye to pinning motives for murder, he might have thrown me out on my assets.

"How's your father?"

"I haven't actually been in touch with him since the early morning hours, Jack. I left him on Ted's boat, anchored in the middle of Pirate's Cove, with a stern note commanding him to remain on board, out of sight."

"Will he do that?"

"I also took the Boston whaler to shore with me."

"Ah." The seventy-seven-year-old face creased into a grin. "And your father has never been a strong swimmer, as I recall. He tried to wear a life jacket at a diving competition at the club when he was a child. It took some convincing by the volunteer swim coach, who happened to be me, to persuade him that diving with a life preserver on was a bit like diving headfirst into a wall of wet cement. Well, enough of your dad." He smiled. "Heaven knows, we've all had enough of your dad. How are you, my dear?"

"I'm grateful for your intercession with the other trustees, so I could have these days off." When his eyes narrowed slightly, I leaned forward to say, before he could beat me to it, "Jack, I know. The trustees have to think of the good of the Foundation; you can only afford to be understanding for a limited amount of time. If I'd taken a loan from this bank, you'd expect me to pay it back, and if I couldn't, I'd expect you to foreclose. Well, when I became the director of the Foundation, you trustees expected me to fulfill my obligations, my father notwithstanding. If I can't do that, I'll expect you to . . . foreclose."

His mouth pulled downward in distress.

"Jack, don't worry, don't apologize. Besides, I fully intend to get this business cleared up and to be back on the job soon. I may suffer from guilt through association with him, but I'll be damned if either of us will suffer from undeserved guilt. My father's not guilty, but somebody else is. Will you help me find out who that is?"

He looked surprised, but didn't refuse.

"I've been doing a lot of thinking about the murders, Jack, and I've come to the conclusion that we're all looking in the wrong direction for a motive. Forget sabotage, forget racial motivations. Consider the possibility that rather than wishing to destroy the project, somebody desperately wants it to succeed."

His look of surprise grew.

"Explain," he commanded.

I outlined my thoughts for him.

But when I finished, he was shaking his head. "I can't argue with the logic of your hypothesis, Jennifer," he said, "but I can't think of anyone associated with the project who is that desperate for it to succeed. It's true that Betty and Pete Tower have a lot riding on their café, but Pete is not the total fool he seems. Actually, he's rather savvy about money. Quite apart from the property they put up as collateral for their construction loan, they have a couple of rental properties that produce a steady income. If the harbor fails, they'll be down, but they won't be out, Jenny."

"Oh." I couldn't keep the disappointment out of my voice. "But at church Sunday, Betty sounded frantic about opening their café on time and making their loan."

"Betty always sounds frantic."

"Yes," I said regretfully. "But what about Web, Goose?"

"Oh, them!" Jack waved a slim hand as if those two men were negligible concerns. "Have you stopped to think that Port Frederick is not exactly awash in architects and contractors, especially good, experienced ones? Web talks a big game, but he's too conservative to venture far outside of town. Hell, he doesn't have any competition, to speak of! He'll be happy and successful right here in town."

"That's what you say."

"In the privacy of his banker's office, that's what he says, too. Take my word for it, Webster Helms will bask in the local glory of Liberty Harbor, but he won't use it to catapult himself to national fame. There's more than enough work for him here, and he knows it better than anybody."

"But what if the harbor fails?"

"He's still the only game in town."

"I guess so." I straightened my shoulders to keep them from drooping with disappointment. "And Goose? Isn't he desperate to prove he can still handle the big jobs?"

Jack shook his head at me. "As my old grandmother used to say, Pshaw! Jennifer, Goose is just going through a midlife crisis a little late; that's all that's wrong with him. Besides, he has insurance, you know, and the developers can't hold him responsible for delays that are clearly not his fault."

I sighed. "I guess it's pretty ridiculous to think that Barbara Schneider would do anything more than metaphorically kill to get reelected."

"She's ambitious, but not that ambitious."

"Ted Sullivan?" I ventured. "Hardy, Mary Eberhardt?"

"Are you looking for a murderer? Or a sacrificial lamb?"

I threw up my hands in exasperation. "I know it's awful of me to suspect these nice people. But damn it, Jack, they do stand to gain from the development of Liberty Harbor!"

"You mean Ted's going to make more money because renewed prosperity will improve the real-estate market? As motives go, Jennifer, that strikes me as a cousin thrice removed. And I have to tell you that I'm ashamed of you for impugning the motives of the Eberhardts. They are seeking the welfare of their black brothers and sisters, they are not seeking self-aggrandizement. And you ought to apologize for thinking otherwise."

I looked at him, startled.

Then I put my head briefly in my hands.

"Oh God," I said miserably, "you're absolutely right. What am I doing? These people are decent, upstanding citizens of this city. How can I even think of them as murder suspects?"

His stern expression relaxed. "You're trying to keep your father from being lynched by the decent, upstanding citizens of this town who are still so angry at him for going bankrupt and putting them out of work that they would seek revenge by pinning on him a crime he did not commit. I understand."

I rose from the chair to shake his hand. "Thank you for putting things in perspective for me, Jack. Thanks for setting me straight before I inflicted lasting damage to some good reputations."

He waved away my gratitude.

"Don't let them ruin your reputation, Jennifer," he said strongly. "Or what little is left of your father's."

He escorted me to the door.

"By the way, Jennifer, just in case you're wondering: if Liberty Harbor should fail, God forbid, this bank will not follow it down the tubes. We are delighted to be sponsoring so many loans to the people involved with it, but we are not dependent on that project for the continued health, wealth and happiness of our stockholders."

I flushed.

He winked.

I fled.

chapter
25

It was one thing to follow Geof around the police station, passively experiencing a murder investigation, almost enjoying it, in fact, since it was a fascinating process and the victims were nobody I mourned. How different it felt to be aggressively involved. With every question I asked, I ran the risk of losing friends and making enemies, and of combining all the answers to those questions into wrong, even hateful and potentially harmful conclusions. Who did I think I was, anyway?

I was my father's daughter, a fact that could have been interpreted in less than flattering ways which I chose to overlook.

Nevertheless, I drove away from the bank feeling tired, discouraged, humbled, depressed. Which was more or less how Geof had described himself as feeling during the low moments of an investigation when all roads were cul-de-sacs that led back to the beginning.

I returned to the shoreline where I had moored the dinghy, I hauled the rest of my gear to the little boat, locked my car and rowed back to the *Amy Denise*. Halfway there, I remembered that I had neglected to stop at a grocery for supplies. I could only hope that my father had not already consumed the contents of the grocery sacks I'd helped him load the night he moved onto the boat. It seemed doubtful that he could have eaten all of it already: caviar, two pounds of Brie, imported pâté, biscuits in tins from England, fresh blueberries, raspberries and strawberries, chocolates, macadamia nuts, beef tenderloin, veal cutlets, new potatoes, Belgian ham, Spanish olives, Greek bread and Russian vodka. He'd been disappointed when we couldn't locate any imported French butter; but I'd assured him there was margarine aboard, left over from the lobster feast that Geof and I had enjoyed. "Oh well," my father said, followed by one of the few parental homilies he'd ever uttered: "We can't have everything we want in life, Jennifer. Sometimes we must make do with what the fates provide." To which he'd added thoughtfully, "That's a good lesson to remember, my dear."

Well, the fates had provided me with a gooney bird of a father. I rowed to the boat, tied the dinghy to the swim ladder, climbed up, awkwardly hauling my gear with me, swung my legs over the rail, stood on the aft deck and commenced to make do.

"Dad," I said midway through dinner, "what did the police ask you before I got to the station last night?"

His consciousness seemed to float in from a great distance, perhaps from California. "Ask me?" He looked puzzled. "I told them how lovely the coast, the other coast, is this time of year. The sea lions come up, you know, and at other times, the whales."

"I'm sure you did, Dad. I'm sure it is. Dad, did they want to know where you were last Sunday? Where you were a week ago Friday, and the following Saturday? Did they ask you questions like those?"

"What is today, Jennifer?"

"Monday."

"We usually go to one of our clubs on Mondays, you know. There's dancing on the patio until midnight, and oh, you'd adore the orchestra, I feel certain you would. You do like to dance, don't you, Jennifer?"

"Why were you at the church yesterday, Dad?"

"Jennifer," he said, unexpectedly alert, "you can't expect me to remain on this boat all the time. Besides, it was an excellent chance to present my views to the media."

"Views?"

"Yes, about how the town ought to rename that place Cain Harbor."

"Dad! You didn't say that to a reporter, did you?"

"No." He was put out. "They all ran off after that nasty short loud man before I had the opportunity."

"But how did you know about the event at the church?"

"I picked up a paper at the marina when I docked there Sunday morning. And I rented a car to drive into town." He was answering questions more directly than in all the thirty years I'd known him. I pressed him while I had him.

"So when did you leave the church, Dad?"

He poked a forkful of veal into his mouth. I hoped he could remember the question long enough to chew, swallow, then deliver an answer; but I suspected I'd lost him. When his mouth was once more empty, he said to me, "Do you know, Jennifer, I saw oodles of people I knew at that church. Don't you think that's odd? But nobody was around after the service; I looked for all my old friends, but they'd gone."

"I'm sorry." I was, too, because I wanted somebody who recognized him to have seen him leave that church before Atheneum McGee was killed in it. I made another stab at a pertinent theme.

"You came to my office last Monday morning, but when did you actually get to town, Dad?"

He twirled a forkful of noodles into a fat, glistening ball and popped it whole into his mouth.

"Dad?"

"That weekend," he said vaguely.

"You mean Sunday? Or do you mean Saturday? Where were you a week ago Saturday, Dad?"

He sighed and laid down his fork, obviously humoring

me. "I told you, dear, I was staying at that motel where they don't even furnish coffee and croissants and *The Los Angeles Times* in the morning. And let me think, I believe that after the groundbreaking ceremony, I stopped at The Buoy for a drink. Ran into some old friends there, too, but they were in a hurry to get someplace else. In a hurry is a funny thing to be on Saturday, don't you think?"

I laid down my own fork and stared at him.

"You were at the groundbreaking ceremony?"

He smiled, but it held regret. "Do you think it was wise to wear black linen in the middle of the day? I would have thought it more appropriate for evening and for cooler weather, but then I suppose you know best about those things. Perhaps I'll ask your stepmother, if you'd like me to."

"But I didn't see you there. Were you standing on the shore with the other spectators?"

"Oh my, no!" He was amused. "No, I had a rental car, you see, so I drove up to that old lover's leap. It's certainly become filthy, I must say, but one gets such a marvelous view of the whole bay from up there."

"Lover's leap?"

"Yes, dear, I wanted to see all the action."

"You wanted to see all what action?"

"Jennifer, is there more veal? Really, you're almost as good a cook as your mother, although one would never have guessed it from those dreadful grilled cheese-and-tomato sandwiches you used to burn as a child."

"What action, Dad? Why were you expecting action?"

"And a little more noodles, if you please."

"*Dad.*"

He looked at me, plainly exasperated. "All right then," he said, "I'll get it myself. Honestly, this liberation business is all right, but not in a man's home."

My father rose stiffly from the table to fetch a second helping. I remained, dumbfounded, at the table. For the first time in my life, I wondered if his famous vagueness was affected to further his own devious ends. The night before,

Geof had laughed and said, "Trying to question your father is like trying to pin down a cloud. Just when you think you've got it, it floats off in another direction."

He returned to the table in wounded silence and thumped down his plate with unnecessary force. I'd never get anything out of him now; he was angry, or pretending to be. And I was too tired to care. I washed the dishes when we finished, dried them and secured them in the cupboards. Then, after offering a "good night" to which there was no reply, I descended to the forward cabin. My father had tossed his life preserver on my bunk. I picked it up to fling it aside, but changed my mind and held it for a moment in my hands.

My father, I thought, wanting to wear a life preserver in a diving competition. My father, wearing a life preserver the night before at Liberty Harbor, so he looked like a bald weightlifter. My father, whose only real life preserver at the moment was a daughter who wasn't helping much.

I laid the preserver on the other bunk, crawled into my own bunk and was quickly asleep. Toward morning, I came abruptly awake. I threw off my sheet, reached over for that life preserver and crowed: "I'll be damned, so *that's* why!" And then the full meaning of what I had just realized struck me. After that, I didn't sleep so well.

I could hardly wait for morning.

chapter
26

It was a waste of time, and I knew it; worse, it would distract me from my far more important goal which was the clearing of my father of all suspicion. Nevertheless, I wanted to find out if my midnight hunch about the life preserver was correct. Besides, I was getting nowhere in my own investigations; everybody I suspected seemed to be innocent of truly murderous motives. Maybe if I took my mind off my own problems for a while something brilliant would come to me.

In the morning, after a breakfast that was cordial, if quiet, I rowed back to shore and my car. By midmorning, I stood at the reception desk of the Port Frederick *Times,* hoping to God that nobody would recognize me as Jimmy Cain's daughter.

"Do you keep a morgue?" I inquired of the young man on duty. He wore thick glasses of the type that contacts have almost rendered obsolete; I was probably only a dim figure to him. I said, "I want to look up some articles from a few years back."

"Well, not what you'd call a morgue like at a big city paper," he admitted. "I mean, you'd have to go through

151

stacks and stacks of papers, 'cause we don't have anything on microfilm yet. The fire department says we're a fire hazard, but I doubt it. None of our stories are hot enough to catch fire."

I peered into his glasses to see if he was joking. A squinting twinkle said he was. I grinned at him and he grinned back. "That way," he said, pointing a thumb over his shoulder. "All the way to the back, down the steps to the basement. Ask Hilda to help you."

"What does Hilda look like?"

"She looks like the only person in the basement," he said.

"Thank you." Keeping my head down and hiding my face by pretending to scratch my nose, I followed his directions, walking as quickly as if the floor were, indeed, afire.

"What year you want, honey?" asked Hilda, the only person in the basement. She was old and yellowed like the papers that surrounded her. They were piled thickly, but neatly, to the ceiling. She added, in a smoker's voice, "I can get to the last five years pretty easy, but anything before that is a bitch."

"Just two years ago," I told her. "February. I don't know the exact date."

She drew deeply on a cigarette, then flipped her ashes to the floor. No wonder the fire department thought the place was a hazard. Hilda caught me staring at the dead butts that littered the floor around her desk. Like the receptionist, she had a twinkle. "When you're my age, honey," she said in a voice that crackled like old leaves, "you tend to nod off when you least expect it. That's why I don't keep an ashtray. Keeps me awake, wondering if I'm gonna cremate myself." She drew on the cigarette again, so it glowed live and fiery at its tip.

"It's got me feeling pretty wide awake," I told her, and she grinned behind the smoke. Maybe the boy upstairs was her son; maybe he wore those thick glasses so he wouldn't have to see his mother set the house on fire.

She rose slowly by placing her palms on her desk and pushing herself up. Then she led me back into the paper jungle.

"Here," she said, pausing before a stack that looked identical to every other stack. Hilda, evidently, filed by the intuitive system. She said, "This here's what you want. This whole pile is your year, just start at the top—that's December—and work on down. I'll get you a step stool. Just throw 'em down on the floor here 'til you get to February. Ought to be down there near the bottom if it still comes after January."

She wheeled a step stool toward me, then started to walk away.

"Hilda," I said, "you won't nod off, will you?"

"Ain't my day to die," she said.

"From your mouth to God's ears."

By the time I reached February, I was black with newsprint. My hands were stained and the newsprint had rubbed off on my shorts and shirt; even my legs were streaked. By this time, I was down from the ladder and seated on the basement floor. One by one, I skimmed the headlines of all the pages of all the papers starting with February 28, and going backward.

In the evening paper of Feb. 13, I found what I was looking for: LOBSTERMAN MISSING; PRESUMED DROWNED. The Coast Guard, it said, had come upon Lobster McGee's boat just that morning, shortly after it was seen motoring out to where everybody knew that Lobster strung his traps. Somebody on board the Coast Guard cutter had noticed that nobody waved back when they waved at Lobster McGee's boat, and that was odd; even crochety old Lobster would spare a wave for passing mariners. Sensing something out of the ordinary, the Coast Guard had approached, only to find the boat full of lobsters but empty of Lobster. They knew he'd taken the boat out that morning, because he'd been seen by other lobstermen on their way out to their territories. And they knew it was pretty rough water that morning, the kind that requires an experienced lobsterman to hook and winch his pots without tumbling overboard. Lobster had, nonetheless, gone over, that was clear to the Coast Guard. His gaff was still hooked in the nearest pot, so he'd probably gone in while he was in an awkward position of trying to pull the pot in toward the boat. Then most likely he'd knocked his head against the side of the boat, and in that rough water, that was all she wrote. It could happen; it had happened to Lobster. Lobstering was never easy; and sometimes it wasn't even safe. It was a bad morning for going out, but lobstermen have to go out, and Lobster had paid for the tough dedication of his trade.

It took me another half hour to pile the newspapers back up into their original neat stack. On my way out I thanked Hilda for staying awake. She grinned beyond her veil of smoke and flipped an inch of ash to the floor.

"Are you related to the boy at the reception desk, Hilda?"

"That's my kid all right." She shook her head. "Got eyes like a mole, but he's a nice kid. Listen, you might want to hose yourself off in the bathroom right across there." She pointed the cigarette toward a door in the opposite wall. "It's my private john," she said with that familial grin. "'Cause ain't nobody here but little old Hilda."

I thanked her again, then took her suggestion. Her bathroom was as tidy as her morgue, and I carefully rinsed the sink when I was through.

On the first floor again, I ducked my head as I walked quickly across the hardwood floor, between desks and file cabinets.

But not quickly enough.

"Jenny?" A male voice behind me sounded excited. "Is that you, Jenny? Where's your father? We need to talk to him! Jenny Cain!"

I was even with the reception desk.

"Run!" whispered Hilda's boy. As I did, he stood up and started to walk around his desk, but stumbled right in the path of the reporter who was bearing down on me. I turned back long enough to hear the reporter curse and to see Hilda's boy lying sprawled on the floor, his face turned toward the door, that grin plastered across it. His glasses remained safely on his desk where he'd laid them. "Go!" he mouthed at me.

I went, making it to my car, then off and away before Clark Kent could turn into Superman and fly after me.

Hilda's boy might be wrong about one thing, if *I* was right about another: the *Times* did indeed have a hot story that might set the joint briefly aflame. And it didn't have anything to do with their current quarry, James D. Cain III.

I stepped on the gas and drove above the speed limit to Liberty Harbor. Now I knew how Geof must feel just before closing a case. Only I was going to close this one by opening it again.

I parked behind Lobster McGee's old house, out of sight of Goose Shattuck and his construction crew.

The house was deserted, having not, as yet, fallen prey to the reconstructionists and the decorators and the historians. It stood this morning in all its decrepit glory, more a Halloween spookhouse than a future center of culture and nostalgia.

It was a dingy gray, but then every house along the coast is dingy gray unless you paint it regularly. The porch sagged; the windowsills looked as if they could hardly support the weight of what little glass was left in them; old newspapers hung around the bottom of the balustrades like pets clinging to the legs of their master; the front-door screen hung on one hinge like a drunk on a lamppost.

The front door itself was locked, but that posed no problem because most of the glass was broken out of the wide windows beside it. All I had to do was remove one shoe and tap out the remaining glass in one of the windows. It fell lightly to the wood floor within the house.

I took the jacket I had carried from my car and stretched it over the bottom of the window to protect my legs and rear from glass, and I climbed through, pulling the jacket in with me. I let it drop out of sight on the floor.

The place was a wreck, but probably not much worse than when Lobster had lived there. Because of the broken windows, sand and salt had blown in along with some leaves and miscellaneous trash; but it all looked right at home with the basic layer of filth the old man had laid down before he died. Had he ever cleaned up after himself? Or was this the dust of years of not giving a damn for anything but Big Macs and lobsters? It would take someone with a finer eye than mine to see the potential here, and then to pore through the dirt for the golden architectural nugget that was said to lurk in the bones of this old house. I didn't like the house, and hurried through the downstairs rooms to find what I was looking for. I only hoped it was still there and had not been stolen, as had many of the so-called artifacts before the preservationists persuaded Goose to have his guards include this relic in their nightly rounds.

It wasn't downstairs, if it still existed at all.

I climbed the stairs, skipping three at a time in my rush to be gone.

Seven doors opened off the hallway upstairs. I looked in the two bathrooms just long enough to eliminate them as hiding places for the object I sought. Neither was it in the first two bedrooms I looked in. The last bedroom down the hall was locked with a small padlock. I figured it must be Lobster's room, or else the preservationists wouldn't have gone to the trouble of locking it. I tested the strength of the wood in the door with my hands, then a foot.

I went back downstairs for a log from the vast stone fireplace. Then I hauled the log back up the stairs and rammed it through the door. After that, it was easy to get in the room. I walked through the huge hole I'd made in the door and stared around.

"Breaking and entering," I said to myself. "Assault on a door with a deadly weapon. You're as crazy as your father, and twice as dangerous. If Geof ever finds out you did this, he will find you a room in a jail."

The McDonald's sacks had been removed. I don't know who counted them. Lobster's heavy walnut furniture remained—a massive double bed, matching chest of drawers, a dressing table with a yellowed mirror, and two straight-backed chairs, one of them drawn up to the window where the telescope looked out to sea. Old newspapers had blown into the corner.

I searched every inch of that crusty room and failed to find what I was looking for: a fat orange life jacket, the one that gave him the look of a stuffed sausage every lobstering season, the one he wore under his clothes to hide the truth about a proud, tough old sailor who couldn't swim.

But was I wrong?

I stepped to the broken window to peer through Lobster's telescope. I had to bend awkwardly to look toward the harbor where his old lobster boat was tied to one of the docks. The scope brought the boat into wonderful closeup, including the detail of the lifeline that Lobster had jerryrigged along the inside edge of the boat. At the bow, a metal hook dangled from the line, waiting to join up with the metal eye on the life preserver that Lobster McGee would have worn every time he went out on that boat. And if the old man always wore a life jacket and hooked up to the lifeline when he was out in the boat, that meant that if he'd been knocked overboard accidentally or fallen out of the boat, the jacket would have kept him afloat for a good long time. At the least, the Coast Guard would have found his body, still hanging from the lifeline, soon after the accident happened.

The old man didn't drown in an accident.

He was murdered.

Even without the proof of the well-worn jacket I should have found in that room, I felt I could convince Geof. But murdered by whom? Why? Exactly how?

My theory ended where those questions began.

I tried to swing the telescope to starboard, but found it locked in place. A quick fumble with the catch loosened it. Now I could see Goose down at the site, waving his arms at some of his men. And there was Webster Helms, strutting into his rebuilt shack. I swung the scope again, this time finding what was left of the old pier where my committee had dived into the bay. And then I swung it still further around and, in so doing, found myself dropping naturally into the chair beside the window. Now I realized that it was pulled up to the telescope so that a person using it could sit comfortably in this position, staring in this direction. And what I saw from this position was lover's leap. I watched a young couple in a Datsun 210 drive up and park. She was a pretty brunette with a few dark hairs between her eyebrows.

He turned off the ignition, took his hands off the wheel and put them on her blouse . . .

I looked away.

Sitting here, Lobster McGee might have observed any number of secret things that the people involved would not have wished anyone to see. Did he sit here night after night in lobstering season and day after day in off season, eating his hamburgers and peering through his telescope at other people's private lives? Did he see something that somebody didn't want him to? Something so private, so secret, so *wrong* that they killed him for his knowledge?

I stood up, pushed the telescope away, and stared sightlessly down at the old lobster pound. On this hot day its stench rose up to me through the broken window.

"I'm sorry, Dad," I said. "I'm not much help to you, but I think I can help old Lobster McGee rest easier in his grave."

The house was haunted to me now. I scrambled out of it, returned to my car and drove to the police station.

chapter
27

"Lobster McGee was murdered?" Ailey Mason looked at me like a juggler who's just been handed one too many balls. We were standing in the hallway outside of Geof's office, which Ailey was blocking with his short, wide body. He stared at me resentfully. "What the hell are you talking about? That was, what? Four years ago? Three?"

"Two." I tried to walk around him, but he moved with me. "You're not on the football team anymore, Ailey. You don't have to block for the quarterback. Let me see him, please. Now."

Grudgingly, he moved aside. I opened the door and received a much more welcoming smile from the detective inside. Before I could say hello, Ailey announced my mission.

"You're not going to believe this, but she's got this theory that old Lobster McGee—you remember him?—was murdered. She wants us to drop everything to figure out who committed this alleged murder five years ago."

"Two," I said. "I don't want you to drop everything. I just want you to know."

"Hi," Geof said. "Come on in. Ailey, sit."

The younger detective obeyed. I reached across Geof's wide metal desk to kiss and be kissed, then I took the remaining chair across from him. He looked at me expectantly, as if waiting to be entertained.

"How's your father?" he asked.

"Safely restrained."

"I think that would take a straitjacket, but never mind. What's this about Lobster McGee? Another murder to solve is just what we need around here, you know."

"I know," I said apologetically. "I was on the boat last night with my dad, Geof. And in the middle of the night, I woke up with the solution to one of the mysteries about Lobster McGee."

"You not only know he was murdered, but you know who did it?" Ailey was disbelieving.

"Not that mystery," I admitted. "I figured out why he used to look so stout in the winter and so thin all summer. Now wait a minute, this is more important than it sounds! Do either of you remember how Lobster seemed to put on a lot of weight every lobster season, only to lose it when the season ended?"

Geof shook his head in the negative, but Ailey admitted to having noticed that phenomenon.

"Well," I said, "the reason is that during the lobstering season, the old man wore a life jacket under his clothes. He couldn't swim! And I guess he was so vain that he couldn't bear for any of the other lobstermen to know, so once he put the darn thing on, he had to keep it on all day long. He wore it under his clothes, Geof."

"How do you know?"

"Well, I don't know," I admitted. "At least not in the sense of having a signed affidavit from the old man himself. But I *know.*" I explained how my unconscious had made the deductive leap from the memory of the barrel-chested silhouette of my father to the memory of the seasonally barrel-chested Lobster McGee. And I told them about having spied the lifeline through the telescope.

"I won't ask how you got into Lobster's bedroom," Geof said.

"Just as well."

"So what if he wore a life jacket?" Ailey broke in. "What's it got to do with his death?"

I explained that, as well.

By the time I was through, Geof was staring at me thoughtfully and Ailey was gratifyingly silent.

"So," Geof said, "did somebody take him out in the boat and toss him over? Or did they kill him someplace else? Is his body on land, or at the bottom of the sea? And why would anybody kill that old hermit?"

I told them then about the telescope.

Geof's eyes lit up. "That's very interesting, Jenny. What do you think happened on top of that hill the week that Lobster died? What did he see that somebody didn't want him to see?"

"Well," I said, "it is a lovers' lane."

"You think maybe somebody parked up there who didn't want to be seen?" Geof stared at me with heightened intensity. "Jenny, you say the telescope was turned to the sea when you found it, and locked into position?" I nodded. "And yet the chair was situated so the telescope was awkward to use when you looked through it at anything other than the top of the hill?" Again, I nodded. "Then who turned that telescope around?"

"The preservationists?" Ailey ventured.

"No," Geof said, "I think it was whoever killed Lobster. That person locked that telescope in place so no one would cotton to Lobster's favorite hobby. But assuming he did spy on somebody, how would they find out about it?"

"Blackmail," I said.

"Bingo." He turned to Ailey. "Get a team over to that house and go over it as if McGee had just died today. I know it's an exercise in futility, but check the damn dust for fingerprints, the whole works. And keep this quiet, will you? Take a couple of unmarked cars and park out of sight of the construction site."

Ailey looked sourly at me and pulled a long face. "Thank you so much." He trudged out of the room.

Geof smiled at me. "You may have a future as a detective."

"Good. I may need a job. So tell me, how are you doing on Port Frederick's more recent homicides?"

He shifted in his chair. "Jenny, when Reich came to your office that Friday before he was killed, whom did you inform of his visit and his threats?"

"I called Goose to ask him about Reich, but I didn't actually tell him that Reich had threatened the project. And I called all the other members of the committee to tell them, but I didn't give Reich's name."

"What did you say about him?"

I tried to recall my words. "I guess I said that a man had come to my office. Accused me and the Foundation of contributing to the death of his son. Made threats of revenge against the project."

"That's it?" He looked disappointed. "You're sure you didn't give out his name?"

"Positive."

"Did you tell them he worked at the harbor?"

"No. Well, I may have mentioned construction." I smiled. "They all wanted to know why I was so scared of this stranger, and I told them he was a giant of a man, a construction worker, and they'd be shaking, too."

The disappointment vanished from the detective's face. He leaned back in his chair as if satisfied. "Any one of them could have identified him from that description, Jenny."

"What? How?"

"Think about it," he instructed. "How many construction jobs are going on now? Apart from a few homes, the harbor is the only game in town. They don't call us depressed for nothing, you know. And how many giants does Goose have working for him? Even given the size of some of those bruisers, nobody to match Reich. He stood head, shoulders and hard hat above the other workers, I'd say."

I was horrified. "Oh Geof." My hands came to my face,

but they couldn't cover my dismay. "I led his killer to him! Wait a minute! You're talking as if you think his death was tied to those threats against the project. And that means you think he was killed because somebody thought he might stop or delay it, don't you?"

"Yes."

"Well," I said, "great minds. I think so, too."

"I'm now working on the assumption that somebody killed Reich by accident when they tried to scare him into leaving the harbor alone. And since your committee alone knew of those threats, I'm afraid it has to be one of you." He smiled apologetically. "Them."

"What about Atheneum?"

"He was also killed because he represented a threat to the project."

"But he'd agreed to go after his relatives for the money!"

"Who says so, Jenny?" Geof leaned forward and his chair cracked. "I've tried to pin down exactly who got that agreement out of him and nobody can say for sure. Betty Tower says Ted Sullivan told her about it, and Ted says he heard it when Pete and Jack Fenton were talking in the hall by the water fountain, and they both claim they heard it from Hardy, and he doesn't know who told him but he knows *he* didn't persuade McGee, and his wife thinks . . ."

"I see what you mean." I held up a hand to stop the flow of conflicting, confusing testimony. "But I've been asking around, Geof, and there's nobody on my committee who has a strong enough motive for wanting the project to succeed. Oh, sure, we all want it, but I'd swear nobody has a motive strong enough to kill for."

"You've been checking?" He gave me a look. "So that's why you're taking these days off. I guess you know my official police opinion of that."

"I guess I do."

"I guess you don't give a damn about my official police opinion."

"I guess I don't."

"All right." He sighed. "Now tell me what you know."

I conveyed the information I'd gleaned from my phone

call to the Federal Reserve, my lunch with the Towers and Web, and my interview with Jack Fenton at the First. When I was done, I spread my hands wide. "So there you have it . . . nine good suspects, no good motives."

"But you're assuming the killer wants the project to go forward because of something he or she *desires*," he said slowly.

"What else?"

"Desire implies future, Jenny. What about the past?"

"What about it?"

"Maybe there's something that somebody on the committee wants to hide from his or her past?" He looked at me meaningfully, but still it took a moment for me to grasp it.

"My God," I breathed. "Lobster McGee's murder."

He nodded, saying nothing.

Now I wondered if he was only being tactful in limiting the suspects to the committee. I wondered, as well, where my father was during the second week of February two years ago.

chapter
28

"Your stepmother keeps our social calendar," my father said that afternoon when I rowed back out to the *Amy Denise* to ask him. "She would know. You had better ask her, dear."

It was a more direct answer, by far, than he usually emitted, but that was only because I had asked it, with various permutations, no fewer than seven times. He stayed on the same wavelength with me long enough to inquire, "Why do you ask, dear?"

I saw the gray eyes go foggy and drift out to sea.

"Because," I said clearly, "a man was murdered that week and I want to know if you have an alibi."

"Do you know," he said fretfully, "I have reached the point on this boat at which I do believe I would welcome a night at the Ramada."

"Was that a joke, Dad?"

He focused briefly. "I beg your pardon?"

"Never mind."

I fixed him a martini, broke open a can of macadamia nuts, stuck a small roast in the oven and rowed back to shore. My back and shoulder muscles were developing nicely; at this rate I would qualify for the women's Olympic sculling team in no time. From the nearest pay phone, I placed a credit card call to my stepmother, Miranda. Before meeting her, I had thought that only stepmothers in fairy tales had names like Miranda, but she was all too real.

"Hello, Randy," I said. "It's Jennifer."

"Yes, dear," she said brightly. Miranda was five years older than I. "Is your father there with you?"

"No, he's . . ." It would take too much effort to explain. "Miranda, do you happen to have retained your social calendar from two years back?"

"Of course, dear." She didn't seem surprised at the question. But then, this was a woman who lived with my father; she had probably long since ceased being surprised at anything. "I keep all our records for tax purposes. I wouldn't want the IRS to steal one dollar more of your father's hard-earned money than they absolutely have a right to."

"My father's hard-earned money? Which money is that, Miranda?" I put my hand to my forehead. "I'm sorry. Never mind. Listen, if you can put your hands on the calendar, it would help Dad. I'll explain later, if you don't mind. Would you look for it now? I'll wait."

She dropped the receiver without a word—which was probably what I deserved—and was gone for several minutes. When she returned, she was polite as ever to her snippy, resentful stepdaughter. "Yes, dear, now what is it you need from the calendar?"

"Look up February, please."

"I have it here."

"Second week."

"Um. Yes, here it is. Oh, don't you remember, Jennifer? That was the week we were in Port Frederick for your sister's birthday. Don't you remember the mixup? She thought we were coming the following week, and when we arrived, she and her whole family had left for Puerto Vallarta. We stayed with you for a night, remember, and then you had to leave suddenly on business." She managed to say all that in a sincere voice that gave not a hint that she knew perfectly well that Sherry had left me holding the bag, and that I had taken all I could before escaping on the first flight, and the first pretext, to New York.

How could I have forgotten that awful week?

"Please," I said weakly, "don't tell me you were in town that whole week. I thought you left right after I did."

"Oh no, dear. Your father wanted to visit with his old cronies." Her laugh started as a clear, bell-like sound, but then it cracked. "Only his old cronies weren't so eager to see him." She covered up that peek into reality by adding quickly, "Why dear? Is it important?"

I forced a laugh. "Life and death, Miranda."

Her melodious laughter floated to me from California. I pictured her, fresh, tanned and voluptuous—and five years older than I—holding the phone in one hand and a glass of white wine in the other. "Oh Jennifer," she trilled, "you're so theatrical sometimes . . . like me. Someday, you'll appreciate how much alike we are in some . . ."

"Thanks so much, Randy." I swallowed. "And Dad sends his love."

"Kisses to him," she said. "Kissy, kissy to my Jimmy. Bye dear." I hung up before I threw up. I already had a mother. I didn't want another one who was young enough to be my sister. Besides, I already had a sister and she was too much for me as it was.

I leaned my shoulder against the wall of the phone booth. "Oh Dad." I sighed. "Poor Dad. They're gonna hang you in the closet and I'm feelin' so sad."

I wasn't, however, feeling particularly civic-minded. If Detective Geoffrey Bushfield wanted to know where my father was the second week of February two years previously, he could just ask the man himself. That would make him sorry he'd ever inquired. I wondered if my father could so buffalo a prosecuting attorney and a jury that they would acquit him on grounds of self-defense. Theirs.

* * *

Before I left Geof's office that morning, he and I agreed on a strategy that would probably get him fired if his superiors found out about it.

"Jenny," he said, "I want to know what was happening in the lives of your committee members around the time that Lobster died. But if I ask them, or Ailey does, we may alert the killer that we're digging back into Lobster's death. You could talk to them without arousing their suspicions."

"How will I start a conversation about events that happened two years ago?"

"You'll think of something," he said, unhelpfully.

Thus far, I had not. Maybe if I could recall what was going on in the world and this town on that long-ago date, I could devise some conversational gambits. I searched my mind, trying to remember the headlines of stories that had appeared in the February papers I had perused, but couldn't. I had been concentrating on the search for Lobster's obituary to the exclusion of everything else. Still in the phone booth, I sighed again. It looked as if another trip to the *Times* was in order.

I picked up the receiver and dialed again.

"Port Frederick *Times,*" said a male voice. "All the news you want to know and some you don't."

I laughed. "This must be the reception desk."

"Speaking. Woodenly. That's how desks speak."

"I think you're a splinter faction," I returned, and he laughed. "This is Jenny Cain. I want to thank you for helping me escape the clutches of your reporters this morning."

"All in the line of subversive duty."

"I need another favor, uh . . . what is your name?"

"Timothy Isley."

"Son of Hilda?"

"The same."

"Well, Timothy Isley, I need to get back down to that basement to look up some additional articles, and I need to do it without being seen or recognized."

"There is a door," he said, "at the rear of the basement.

We will station our troops there to admit you. Just say the secret pass phrase."

"Which is?"

"Smoking causes cancer in laboratory rats and mothers."

"She'll love that, Timothy, but I'll tell her."

"Thank you. When should we expect you?"

"Fifteen minutes."

"I'll post a guard."

I hung up, feeling conspiratorial.

During the February in question, the United States was accused by a Pan American organization of shipping illegal arms to an embattled Latin American country; the yen rose in value against the dollar; the Italians installed two different governments, one at the first of the month and the second around Valentine's Day; a Beirut businesswoman was kidnapped by terrorists who were variously linked to Israel, the PLO and the Red Guard; a blizzard closed the Denver airport for two days; and a Russian head of state died of ailments associated with old age.

"Hell," I muttered to myself as, once again smeared with newsprint, I sat cross-legged on the basement floor surrounded by the news of many yesterdays. "Why am I going to all this trouble, when I could have used today's paper just as well to find out what was going on two years ago?"

On the local scene that month, Hardy Eberhardt's church sponsored a black leadership forum which was attended by nationally known figures. One of them, when asked about a supposed resurgence of the KKK, said, "These days, racist activity advances our cause, because most white Americans are appalled by it and ashamed of it. It plays into our hands because it produces guilt feelings that encourage white America to give us the next thing we want." She was pictured with her arm linked with Mary Eberhardt who was described as "a leading local champion for minority rights."

In the business section for February 12, I found Ted Sullivan pictured in his role as the newly elected president of the local board of realtors. That same day, the after-luncheon speaker at the Rotary Club was Webster Helms, expounding on "The Architect's Role in Fast-Track Construction." Web told the members that, "architects, engineers, builders, contractors and developers all have an important role to play in streamlining the design, engineering and construction process in order to save time and money while at the same time retaining the quality and integrity of the building. Fast track is the future." He must have had the Rotarians nodding over their cherry cobblers. I wasn't surprised to find Jack Fenton's bank mentioned throughout the business sections that month, and the man himself frequently photographed as he shook variously grateful and beseeching palms.

In that same February, Barbara Schneider was sworn into her second term on a platform of economic revival; she also appeared in photographs of one banquet, two meetings and a ribbon-cutting. "We nearly lost this election to the high-spending Democrats," she was quoted as telling her partisan audience at the banquet, "but we will not lose the battle of the recession to them. This administration will pull this city out of the doldrums, or I will hear from you at the next election." At one of the ribbon-cuttings, I spied the looming figure of Goose Shattuck and the smaller one of Web Helms, they having joined forces on the project as they did so often. Goose and Web were the odd couple physically and in temperament, but Goose got along with the persnickety little architect as few other builders could.

But it was in the police blotter for the twelfth of that month that I came upon the most interesting item by far: One Elizabeth Tower, forty-nine, had been picked up for DWI, booked and released.

"I'll be damned," I breathed. I reread the paragraph to see where she'd been arrested: on the highway overlooking the future site of Liberty Harbor. "I'll be double damned."

The only committee members who were not represented in the papers that month were Pete Tower and Jennifer Cain. Why, I asked myself, was Pete's wife drunk that night? Where had she been, where was she going, what had she done, seen, heard, who was with her, was she alone? And why was she driving that highway, far across town from her suburban home, that night?

I returned the papers to their original stack once again, wheeled the step stool back to Hilda, thanked her again and made for the backdoor.

"Hello!" she called to me. I turned to find her peering at me through a fog of smoke. "A reporter was down here after you left the first time, wanted to know what you was here for. I told him you was mighty interested in one particular month of one particular year."

I tried to keep my face from showing dismay.

"September," she said. "Nineteen forty-five."

I began to laugh.

"Took him three hours," she said, "to rummage through all those back issues. Sure hope he found what he was lookin' for, don't you?"

"Hilda," I said gratefully, "you give a whole new meaning to the Freedom of Information Act."

"Thank you, honey," she said, and coughed. She was still coughing when I closed the door on that stronghold of subversive activity in the basement of the Port Frederick *Times*.

Minutes later, I called Geof from yet another pay phone to apprise him of my latest activites.

"So I'll start with the Towers," I suggested.

"Good. Uh." When he spoke again, he was trying to sound casual, but not succeeding. "Say, Jenny, I might take a run out to see your father this afternoon. Where'd you stash that dingy anyway?"

"I don't think you can find it without me," I lied. "Why don't you wait until tonight? I'll row you out there myself."

"All right," he said slowly, reluctantly.

"Later," I said quickly. Much later.

chapter
29

With all the talk about the French café that Pete and Betty would be opening at the harbor, I tended to forget they were already the proprietors of a couple of franchise taco stands, which must have been the collateral Jack Fenton had mentioned. Or, maybe it was the food they served that gave me amnesia: watery tacos, doughy burritos, tough enchiladas, all slathered with sour cream. That was the dead giveaway: the quality of the food at a Mexican restaurant is always in inverse ration to the amount of sour cream used. The Towers must have owned a dairy; maybe that was one of Pete's little investments on the side. My stomach recoiled at the thought of their imminent ethnic leap from Tex-Mex to French. But who was I to argue with the wisdom of the commercial loan department of the First City Bank? Although I did wonder if the bank had relied too much on economic and not enough on culinary advice.

"May I help you?" asked the youth behind the counter at the first of the two restaurants. She wore a yellow peaked cap that proclaimed, "El Biggo Taco."

"I'm looking for Pete or Betty."

"Try their other place."

"May I help you?" inquired the youth behind the counter at the second restaurant. His peaked cap was orange and it said, "Head Honcho." I gathered he was the manager.

"Betty or Pete around today?"

"Try their other place."

I finally found them at home. Neither of them was wearing a peaked cap, either yellow or orange. Either color would have clashed with the basically flamingo pink decor. Even the robe in which Betty answered the door was flaming pink, and ruffled to within an inch of its life.

"Jennifer?" She looked about as pleased as if I were collecting for a charity. It was early afternoon and she was wearing pink mules—those backless high heel slippers— with pink feathery stuff around the toes. I resolved, if she let me in, to look around the house for the Frederick's of Hollywood catalog. She said, with evident regret, "Well, don't just stand there, Jenny, come on in." She left the front door open. Subtle.

I got as far as the entryway. She draped an arm across the doorway to the living room, effectively blocking my access to the rest of her home. I was rapidly losing the desire to be tactful.

"Jenny," she said, "I hope you haven't come here to enlist our help in support for your father. As Webster said, it's nothing personal, you understand, but we have to think of the good of this town, and your father is not good for this town."

Out the window with tact went my additional original intention to be kind.

"I'm sorry to hear that," I said, smiling gently. "I thought you'd be just the person to give us the benefit of your experience with the law."

She stiffened, so that with her arm still propped against the doorsill, she looked like a store mannequin that some-body had stashed and forgotten.

"What's that supposed to mean?" she said aggressively, but I noticed that she lowered her voice when she said it, and her eyes registered a fear she wasn't able to hide.

I kept my voice silky, my smile on straight. "After all, Betty, it's a matter of public record. I just thought you might be able to give us some good ideas about lawyers and dealing with the police." Ruthlessly, I added an insinuating, "You know." Then on a hunch, I added, "Pete around?"

"For God's sake," she hissed. "Be quiet." The arm came down from the doorsill and her lacquered nails landed on my arm. She brought her face so close I could smell her breath. She'd recently used a mouthwash that was about eighty proof.

"Doesn't Pete know?" I said, forcing myself to keep my eyes fastened on hers. "It was in the paper, Betty. How could he not know?"

"Pete knows what I tell him," she said, and I didn't doubt it. "For Christ's sake, Jenny, I even read the papers to him every day! I got myself home that night, I paid the fine, I called the lawyer, Pete never knew one damn thing about it, and you're not going to tell him now."

Was that a threat? I wondered. Had she made a similar threat to Lobster McGee, and then carried it out?

"Nobody told him?" I said. "Nobody mentioned seeing it in the paper? Come on, Betty, you don't believe that, do you?"

Suddenly there were tears in those eyes that were already red-rimmed from secret drinking. "Yes! I believe it! I do!"

I loosened her fingers from my arm.

"Why don't you tell him, Betty? What could he do? If he loves you, he'll stay with you; if he doesn't, you can make it on your own."

"Can I?" she said bitterly. "What do you know? Did it ever occur to you that maybe I love him?"

"No," I said truthfully, "it never did."

"Don't say anything to him," she begged, suddenly pathetic. "Swear to me you won't tell him."

"You need help, Betty."

"Mind your own goddamned business!" she flared then. "Get out!"

I walked back out through the front door that she had never closed behind me, though it slammed hard enough behind me now. A rustling noise drew my eyes to the right. Pete Tower was on his knees, clipping shrubs.

"Hello, Pete."

His head turned toward me as if it were being dragged that way. His round, bland face was suffused with an emotion that looked like hurt, but might have been hate.

I made it to my car without a misstep, but I was breathing hard when I got there. Without pausing, I started the engine and drove around the corner. I parked, switched off the ignition and leaned my head back against the seat.

Was this how detectives felt when they dipped into the dirty corners of people's lives? Was I causing pain to innocent people—innocent, at least, of murder—in the name of saving my own family's skin? I felt like a loose cannon on the deck of this investigation, but I started the car again, arming myself for the next skirmish.

chapter
30

By the time I reached City Hall, the hourly employees had gone home. But I knew a Type-A workaholic when I met one, so I figured the mayor would be there, laboring late on the city's business.

I walked through the empty lobby of the low, one-story building, then down the long hall to the suite of city offices. Previous mayors stared down from the buff walls, none of them distinguished enough to stare back at. The mayor's secretary had covered her typewriter and punched out, but sure enough, the ranking Republican of Port Frederick was still on the job, on the phone. Her voice floated out to me through the closed door of her office.

Quietly, I opened her door just enough to stick my head in to let her know I was there.

The mayor looked up, startled.

So did Ted Sullivan and Goose Shattuck.

"Oh, sorry," I said. "I thought you were on the phone, Barbara, didn't know you had visitors. Is this a private confab, or is there an advisory committee meeting tonight that I have forgotten about?"

"Jenny," the mayor said overheartily. "Come in."

She was echoed in her enthusiasm by the two men, both of whom rose to offer their chairs. It was an unnecessary bit of chivalry, there being an empty chair between them. I took it, wondering, now that I had three birds in the hand, how I was going to feed them all at one time.

"Nothing private going on here," Goose boomed, then turned red. "We were just shootin' the bull about . . . things."

"Things?" I said.

"Sure," Ted said. "Things. You know. Things."

"Right," I said. "Things."

Barbara smiled graciously. "I can't remember the last time you just dropped in like this, Jenny. Anything special on your mind today?"

How could I find out from all of them what they were each doing the second week of February two years ago without arousing their suspicions? Stalling, I said, "I just dropped by to say hello." The conversation was getting more inane by the second. "Well, actually Barbara, that's not true. All right," I said as if coming to a difficult decision, "we're all friends here, right?"

"Oh yes, Jenny," they assured me, as one.

"Well, friends . . . tell me what folks around town are saying about my dad. Do they think he's guilty of anything more than bad judgment? I came to you, Barbara, because I felt that if anyone would have her ear to the pulse of the city, you would." Speaking of pulses, I fairly throbbed with sincerity.

The mayor avoided my eyes. Nor did Goose or Ted rush to be the first in the competition to answer me.

"Since you're here," Barbara finally said, addressing a corner of her desk, "you might as well know . . ."

"Barbara!" Ted said sharply. "Don't you think . . ."

"Hold on," Goose said, quietly for him. "Maybe we ought to give this some more thought before we . . ."

But the mayor looked squarely at me, ignoring them.

"What the gentlemen are trying to discourage me from saying, Jenny, is that we are gathered here this afternoon to discuss your role on the Liberty Harbor Advisory Committee."

"Are you?" I said.

"Yes. It's nothing personal, you understand, but I'm sure you would be the first to appreciate the importance of the, well, reputable standing of the committee within this community. I'm sure you recognize, as well, the importance of our committee pulling together as one team for the good of the harbor, and therefore the town. Liberty Harbor and Port Frederick come first, as far as the committee is concerned."

"Don't tell me," I said. "Let me guess."

"It pains me to say it," she continued.

"I'm sure it does."

"Now, Jenny." Goose covered one of my hands, which rested on the arm of my chair, with one of his own great paws. I slipped my hand out from under his and placed it in my lap where even he was not likely to chase it.

"It pains *all* of us to say it," Barbara persevered, "but we cannot help but wonder if your continued presence on the committee might not represent a rather indelicate conflict of interest."

Actually, I had been thinking of resigning for the very reason that Barbara put forth: it *was* an indelicate conflict of interest for a daughter to participate in a project that her father was suspected of wanting to destroy. But hearing her say so gave me an idea about getting the information I needed, so I decided to play it dumb. And angry.

"You mean," I said, putting a sarcastic edge on my own thoughts, "that folks might ask why I'm getting involved with a project they think my father wants to destroy?"

"Yes," the mayor said gratefully, "I'm so glad you understand. It's really very decent of you."

"Nothing personal," I said, with increasing bitterness, so that even she began to get my phony message. "Right, Barbara?"

"Right!" Ted said enthusiastically.

"Absolutely," Goose boomed.

"Oh dear," Barbara said, frowning. "Now Jenny . . ."

"I would just like to know," I said steadily, "why I am to

be punished for a crime I did not commit. A crime my father has not been arrested for, accused of, tried for or pronounced guilty of. Why is that?" I was rather pleased with that orderly progression of dangling prepositions, but didn't think I'd say so.

"Frankly," the mayor said, "it's for appearances."

"Well, now Barbara," Ted began to object, but she overrode his finer feelings with ruthless honesty.

"Be realistic," she advised me. "It doesn't take a politician to appreciate the importance of appearances. It is imperative that our committee at least *seem* to present a unified, untarnished appearance to the community in order to preserve the harmony that has marked this project so far."

"Harmony?" I said. "You call that flap over the Unmarked Grave harmony? You call those vigilantes harmony?"

"Jenny," the mayor said then, "we have the votes."

"How many?"

"Let's just call it a majority," she replied.

"Let's not," I said. "Let's call it by name. You, Ted?"

He nodded, reddening and looking away from me.

"Goose?"

Another embarrassed nod.

"The Towers and Webster?"

"Yes," said the mayor. "And I."

"But not the Eberhardts or Jack," I guessed.

"No," she said.

"Well." I rose from my seat and pretended to begin to leave. "It's nice to know who my friends are." Then, as if it had just occurred to me, I whirled on her. "Of course! The election's coming up, isn't it? Are you afraid of what people will think if you don't run my father and me out of town on a rail? Are you that hard up for votes, Barbara? Are you so afraid of losing the next election that you'd sacrifice due process on the altar of your ambition? Almost lost it last time, didn't you? I guess you're not taking any chances this time!" I nearly choked on my own clichés.

"That was two years ago," she said heatedly. "It's a

different picture now. Everybody knows I'm a sure winner. I don't need to take any desperate measures to win."

"Desperate measures?" I said. "What desperate measures did you take two years ago, your Honor?"

"It was only a figure of speech, Jenny, for heaven's sake. Goose, you remember, you were on my campaign committee. It wasn't all that tough a fight. I may not have won by the biggest margin in history, but I did win."

"Hell, I don't remember," he said uncomfortably. "You expect me to remember something from two years ago? I could barely remember my name this morning!" He looked over at Ted Sullivan and forced a laugh. "Two years ago! What were you doing two years ago?"

The realtor seemed to flush beneath his tan.

"Be quiet, Goose," the mayor snapped. I stared at her in surprise. She said to the realtor, "Forget it, Ted."

Ted was shaking his head and looking down at the floor. "It was a tough year," he said softly. "Toughest damn year of my life."

"But you were elected president of the board of realtors," I objected, drawing a furious look from the mayor.

"Yes." His laugh was bitter. "They knew I didn't have anything else to do, wasn't selling anything, might as well be president."

"Oh hell, Ted." Goose was embarrassed again. It was true that Ted wasn't the world's greatest real estate agent, and never had been. "That's ancient history. You're doing great now. Hell, we're all doing better."

Ted glanced at me. "Right. I'm doing fine, aren't I, Jenny? Just ask your friend Geof how many offers I've brought by for him to look at on that house of his. Sold it right out from under his nose, haven't I?"

I looked at the mayor. Her attractive face was pale. I looked back at Ted to see a glance pass between them. My little tantrum seemed to be earning all sorts of unexpected dividends, although I would have sworn I had never before seen a spark of electricity pass between the mayor and the realtor.

Nobody seemed to know what to say next, least of all me. Finally, I improvised. "Well, don't bother with the official vote, friends. I quit." I wheeled and flounced out of the room, nearly knocking Webster Helms on his thin ass.

"This is your idea isn't it, Web, kicking me off the committee? You cooked it up in The Buoy yesterday with the Towers, didn't you? Just another one of your bright ideas, like those damn vigilantes."

"I can't take credit for that, Jenny," he said, somehow managing to sound boastful anyhow. "That was Ted's idea. I just took the ball and ran with it."

"Webster Helms," the mayor called out to him, "if you ever give me the wrong time for a meeting again, just because you know I'll vote against you, I will never appoint you to another committee!"

He flushed and looked apologetic. Some people are gluttons for punishment. And committees. I pushed past him and continued my dramatic stomp out the door.

Once in my car, I tried to sort through the information I'd gleaned from my theatrics and my hours at the newspaper. The mayor had faced a tough election last time, and would face angry voters this fall if the project fell through. Ted was feeling like a professional failure, despite the civic offices he held. And if he wasn't having an affair with the mayor, she surely had sympathetic eyes for him. Webster, according to his own words in the paper, was a believer in the fast-track method of construction which had, more than once, been known to contribute to construction accidents and building failures. And Goose, feeling the need to prove himself once more, had probably underbid the project in order to get it. But what did any of those frailties, idiosyncrasies and bits of gossip have to do with lover's leap, the second week of February, two years ago? The Towers still looked like the best bet, but only because Betty had actually been in the vicinity at the right time. Beyond that, there was nothing to link them to murder or motive.

Well, I still had two friends upon whom to inflict my wiles

and stratagems this evening. I swallowed the lump of guilt which lodged in my throat and drove to the house of the minister of the First Church of the Risen Christ.

I caught husband and wife at home, between church meetings. From their backyard came the sound of children playing.

"Yours?" I inquired of Mary when she brought coffee and sugar cookies into the living room of the neat, two-story brick manse.

She glanced toward the back of the house and smiled. "Everybody's," she replied. "Actually, our three are teenagers, Jenny. I suspect they are driving around tonight, eating up their allowances on gasoline."

We laughed together, comfortable in the shared memories of growing up that transcended race and neighborhood. "Cream?" I held out my cup. She poured for me.

"It's funny that I didn't know that about you," I remarked. "The ages of your children, I mean. I'm not sure I even knew you had three."

"Well, we've probably known each other a long time without really knowing each other. It's something we lose as adults, I think, that capacity for really personal friendships. Our friendships seem to form around work or causes or hobbies, focusing on only one or two elements of our lives, to the exclusion of everything else."

"There doesn't seem to be time to get to know people well."

"That's right."

"Maybe we should try to make the time, Mary."

She looked at me, and smiled. "Maybe we should, Jenny."

Hardy came in from the kitchen carrying a plateful of sugar cookies. He sank easily into an armchair, put the plate on his lap and commenced to empty it. "It's nice to have you visit us, Jenny," he said. "Why haven't we done this before?"

Mary and I exchanged looks and smiles.

"I've never been kicked off a committee before, Hardy," I said lightly.

"Consider it a privilege," he advised me. "I spent most of

my youth trying to gain admittance to important committees. Getting kicked off of them is a luxury I've only recently begun to enjoy."

I laughed. "You do give me a different perspective on things, Hardy."

"Black skin will do that," he said seriously. "Every time."

"Now Hardy," his wife said tartly, "martyrdom will not absolutely guarantee your canonization. He who feels sorry for himself ain't no saint."

He grinned at her, his face lighting with affection.

"Hardy, Mary," I said, putting my cookie on the saucer which also held my cup, "I want you to know how grateful I am to you for being so loyal to me. But I was going to resign anyway."

"Suspected you might," Hardy said, munching. "Bad idea."

I looked up in surprise. "It is? Why?"

"Don't want to let the bastards get you down."

"But it is a conflict of interest, Hardy."

"Life is one long conflict of interests, Jenny, in case you hadn't noticed. Listen to me, Sister Jennifer, you ain't done nothin' wrong nohow, and you don't be takin' no shit from nobody."

"But Hardy." I was laughing, feeling better about the world in general; he was, indeed, a minister to the ailing in spirit. "It's not always appropriate to fight; sometimes the better course of action is to give in gracefully, and wait to fight another day."

I turned to Mary. "Don't you sometimes find in the movement that it is better to accept a loss today in order to win a bigger battle tomorrow? It seems to me that if my father and I bend over backward to accommodate these small, sensitive matters, the community will be more likely to feel sympathetic toward him when it really counts—like if he's arrested for crimes he didn't commit? Mary, isn't that true with the black . . ."

"Yes," she said, "it is, although my husband will deny it to his last sugar cookie."

"Take those phone calls that Hardy and I received last

week." They looked embarrassed. "Hey, we might as well talk about them and take the sting away. Don't you sometimes find that when racial slurs are made public, or when somebody does something like burning a cross on your lawn, it has the effect of turning some public opinion your way?"

"Interesting that you'd appreciate that fact," Mary said. "A couple of years ago, we sponsored a forum on black leadership, and that turned out to be an underlying theme of it: the idea of listening for the chords of sympathy that always break through when decent people are denigrated or abused, and then to play on that sympathy in order to obtain support for future, important concerns."

"I haven't heard much out of you two about the Unmarked Grave since Sunday," I remarked. "Is this an example of that philosophy in action? Are you letting go of that, gracefully, and using the sympathy it engenders, in order to gain something important for the future?"

They looked at each other and smiled.

"You must think us very Machiavellian," Hardy said wryly. "We are flattered at this compliment to our intelligence and farsightedness, but wizards at strategy though we are, we hadn't thought that far ahead. We could hardly have predicted that the cross would end up in a man's chest."

His wife made a distressed sound.

"I'm sorry, honey." He turned back to me. "We still want the grave, Jenny, but it seems a tasteless time to say so."

"But what more do you want?" I pressed. "For yourselves, as black leaders, for the community?"

Again, they looked long at each other, but when the two pairs of eyes turned back toward me some of the directness and frankness had gone out of them.

"We only want the usual," he said vaguely. "More jobs, more recognition, more admittance to the halls of power, more of our legal rights as citizens and our moral rights as people."

But Mary burst our laughing. "And if you believe that,

Jenny, we have some swampland in Florida we'd like to show you!"

"Mary!" he said, trying to look put out, but only looking amused. "Close the closet door before Jenny sees our skeletons!"

"What skeletons?" I said, laughing, too, but without feeling the humor. "Tell me."

"No," Mary said, wiping her eyes, and shaking her head with evident regret, "we can't tell you. But we will, soon, I promise you'll be among the first to know."

"How will I know?"

"Oh," said Hardy, "you'll know . . . everybody will. But I'll tell you this much: it came out of that forum two years ago, the one Mary mentioned. And it's been building since then, like a fire inside us." Indeed, the minister looked suddenly consumed by whatever desire it was that burned within him. Looking at him, listening to him, I was startled, then uneasy. Geof would find this conversation extremely interesting; I only hoped it delivered less than it seemed to promise in potential motives for murder.

"Jenny," Mary said sharply, seeming purposefully to draw my attention away from her husband, "will you have another cookie?"

And that's all I got out of them that evening, though I stayed another half hour: more sugar cookies, no more information.

I drove to the police station to discuss the day's gleanings with Geof, but the sergeant on duty told me that Detective Bushfield had already gone home for the night. I called his home from the police station. Instead of the man, I got the telephone answering machine and heard my own voice asking me to leave my name and number.

"Police recruit Cain, reporting in," I said. "Now leaving my post, will be en route to Pirate's Cove where I will maintain a stakeout until morning. If you come to the shore tomorrow and wave a lantern twice, I will row over to pick you up and take you back to the boat for coffee. Ten-four. Over and out. Or, as my stepmother would say, kissy, kissy."

I hung up, intensely missing him.

"Would you care for a cup of java, Miss Cain?" asked the fatherly sergeant with the drinker's nose.

"I've already drunk enough to keep me awake through a boring lecture," I admitted, "but yes, thank you, Sergeant."

For the next half hour or so, I nursed the strong coffee and wound down from the day by observing the quiet comings and goings of the station at night. By the time I washed out my cup and placed it on the coffee tray by the sergeant's desk, I was ready to return to the boat . . . and bed.

chapter
31

The night seemed unusually dark when I pulled my car up to the shore. For the first time in weeks, the sky was cloudy enough to mask the stars; a hazy ring around the moon promised rain for tomorrow, or sooner. A sudden wind bit into me as I got out of the car, and I felt chilled in my shorts and T-shirt. By staring into the darkness, I could just make out the black shape of the *Amy Denise*.

I picked my way through the rocks and sand to the dinghy, which I had dragged up on land and tied to a tree that morning. When I reached it, I removed my shoes and tossed them into the boat, following them with my purse, suitcase and a small bag of groceries. Then I untied the dinghy and pushed her into the high and lapping tide. Dripping water from the knees down, I climbed in. I reached into the bottom of the boat for an oar to push off with, but my hand grabbed pure air.

"What the . . . ?" Somebody had stolen both oars. I fumbled under the seats only to discover the life jackets were gone, as well.

I was too tired to cuss or care. I merely let out a disgusted sigh, then jerked the engine to life. The loss could have been worse, I consoled myself: the thief could have taken the entire boat.

The dinghy puttered faithfully against the choppy tide. I might not break any speed records on my way back to the *Amy Denise,* but at least I'd get there.

I had my hand firmly on the throttle when a heavy swell rocked the little boat violently. I felt the little engine give a jerk under my hand. I grasped the throttle more firmly, just as the entire engine slid off the stern into the ocean, with me still firmly attached to it. Wildly, I grabbed for the edge of the boat just as we were hit broadside by the first of the larger waves that foretold storms at sea that were coming our way.

Suddenly I was in the water, gagging, flailing, but finally having released the throttle. The faithful little engine sank to the bottom of the cove.

"What the hell?" I spat.

I was too surprised to be frightened. How could this have happened to the world's most reliable boat? One moment I had been securely riding along toward the *Amy Denise* and supper and bed, and the next minute I was swallowing saltwater and treading high swells. I couldn't believe it.

What I had to believe was that somebody had loosened the bolts on the outboard just enough to cause the engine to come loose in rough water. The thief who made off with the oars and life jackets must have wanted the engine, too. Had he changed his mind in mid-theft? Or, had I returned too soon, surprising him in the act and forcing him to flee with his job half done?

The water was very cold and getting rougher.

I treaded water and considered my options. I could ride the tide back to shore, except that the shore was no longer visible to me and I wasn't crazy about the idea of passively allowing the ocean to carry me God knew where.

I craned my neck, trying to keep my face out of the water long enough to find the *Amy Denise* again. She was only a dim shape in the night, but I was a strong swimmer and she looked close enough to reach. And if I couldn't reach her, I could still hope to ride the tide back into shore. I only hoped it wasn't a far distant shore.

Determinedly, I struck out against the tide, and with the first overhand stroke, I knew my effort was doomed. Swimming against the tide is the act of a fool. But I was a fool without any less frightening alternative, and any action seemed better than giving my fate up to the whims of the sea.

And I was frightened, finally.

But too stubborn to admit it.

The swimming was agonizingly difficult. Every forward movement seemed to drag all the breath from my lungs and all the energy from the muscles of my legs and arms and back. But I didn't dare to stop and tread water again, since then I would lose any forward momentum I might have gained. Through stinging eyes, I looked again for the *Amy Denise*.

Her running lights had been switched on. She was moving. Out of the cove. Away from me.

"Dad!" I screamed, and took in a horrible mouthful of saltwater. Silently, my brain continued to scream, "Dad! Don't do this to me!"

My father had chosen this of all nights to haul anchor and go for a spin. My arms and legs continued their frantic, forward movements, but my heart had come to a dead stop.

I caught another glimpse of the departing boat, its graceful shape outlined by its lights in the night.

It wasn't the *Amy Denise*.

It was another boat entirely. There was no other boat in the cove, no other boat in sight. Where was my father?

I did not know how far I had come from the shore, or even if I was still in the cove or now further out in the wider sea. My eyes stung horribly from the salt and were as good as blinded by the pain, the darkness and incessant waves. The horizon had long since disappeared into that blackness where the sea and the land become one. I didn't know when the tide would turn. I didn't want to know.

I tried to look toward the sky, only to be smacked full in the face with a wave that gagged me. When I could open my swollen eyes again, I was dizzy, confused, completely disoriented. There were no lights anywhere, not on the shores of the cove I had purposely selected for its seclusion, not even a moon to guide me.

I concluded I was going to die.

Geof would never know what had happened to me. He would think I'd run away to escape my troubles. Would I be declared dead, like Lobster McGee, with my sister lining up for her share of the spoils?

Like Lobster McGee . . .

The phrase ran through my mind, poking me back to consciousness as the water and my own exhaustion carried me limply along.

Like Lobster McGee . . .

Engines don't just fall off boats, I suddenly thought. Oars and life jackets don't just disappear. Somebody had not wanted me to return safely to the *Amy Denise*. Somebody had not wanted me to keep on living and asking questions. Somebody had sabotaged the dinghy, and they . . .

My father, absentminded as he was, would never have left the cove if he thought I'd be returning to it. He was, after all, my father.

So where was he?

The chill and fear squeezed my heart. Whoever had tried to kill me might be with my father now, and I couldn't save him.

I was so cold I could no longer feel my body.

I was floating in the Atlantic Ocean, alone, at night. I was being murdered . . .

Like Lobster McGee . . .

Leave me alone! I begged my brain. Just let me die in peace!

Lobster McGee! it said to me again.

And suddenly I had it. Suddenly I knew who killed Ansen Reich and Atheneum McGee. And who was killing me. And I would not live to tell Geof about it, and the killer would go free.

With a last burst of desperate fury, I plunged my arms up. Down. Up. Down. One after the other, in a grotesque parody of swimming. Again. Again. Again. I would not be anybody's victim. I would not be killed. I would not. I would not. Not. Not. I struggled until the searing agony in my back and hips and shoulders went away and I felt nothing at all. Maybe my arms continued to move through the waves, maybe my legs continued a spasm of kicking. I couldn't know because I couldn't feel them. Eventually I didn't feel anything.

For a very long time, it seemed, I didn't feel anything.

And then my left palm came down violently and painfully on a rock.

The Good Ship Jennifer Cain had landed.

chapter
32

When I woke up several hours later I was furious with Geof for having pulled all the covers to his side of the bed, leaving me so terribly cold and wet. Wet? And why was the mattress stuffed with rocks and why were the sheets so gritty?

I opened my eyes then and remembered most of it. I didn't recall dragging myself so far up on the beach, out of reach of the grasping fingers of the sea, but somehow I had managed it. Now it was morning, and raining and my body ached as if somebody had run it through a carwash without the car. I knew I had to get to a cop or a telephone, but I didn't know if my body would agree to go with me.

Moaning, hugging my limp arms to my sore ribs, I struggled to my knees in the sand, then to my feet, and ran in a staggering crouch to the shelter of the firs at the edge of the deserted stretch of shoreline on which I had beached the night before. Jesus, I thought, this instinct-for-survival business could kill a person. But I was moving, so I just kept stumbling on until I came out of the trees into a clearing where there stood a car and a miracle.

It was my car. That was the miracle.

Unbelieving, I circled it warily like a dog that's afraid the fox will bite him. How could this be? How could I swim for hours, be carried for miles, only to land a few hundred yards from where I'd launched the dinghy? Had Neptune himself speared me on his trident and tossed me back to shore? Shivering, suspicious, still not thinking straight, I stared around me until I had to admit the humbling truth: this was indeed the cove in which we'd anchored the *Amy Denise* and I had not really swum for hours and been swept for miles. It had only seemed that way to a frightened and out-of-condition swimmer on a dark, lonely night.

At last, the cold and rain cleared the fog from my brain. I trotted quickly to my car and fumbled under the front bumper for the hide-a-key. Within seconds, I was racing down the road, with the heater blasting, in search of the pay phone from which I had called my stepmother only the day before.

My wallet lay in my purse at the bottom of the cove, so I used my credit card number. While I waited through one ring, I stared at the bruise on my left hand where palm had met rock.

"Police. Sergeant Cramer."

"Geof Bushfield, please. It's important."

"Who's this?"

"Jennifer Cain."

"Oh, Miss Cain." Evidently, he'd heard of me via the station grapevine, even if I didn't know him. "I'm sorry, ma'am, but Detective Bushfield's gone. We had us a domestic early this morning down on Seventh, with a probable homicide, and he's on the scene. I could maybe raise him for you . . ." The sergeant's tone said more clearly than any tax referendum editorial could express. "We are overworked and under-manned, ma'am, and we need him right where he is and I sure hope you don't insist."

I thought quickly. What could Geof do with my hunch that I couldn't accomplish in the same amount of time? Besides, when I finally gave him a name, I'd have more of the actual proof he would rightfully demand of me. As for my father . . . in the relatively clear light of morning, I no longer believed he was in danger, and yet . . .

"Tell him I seem to have misplaced my father," I said, knowing Geof would initiate a search for him. "And tell him I'll be in touch later today."

"I'll do it."

"Thank you."

He hung up before I did.

I looked at my watch, which had taken a licking but kept on ticking. It was much too early to make the other phone calls I had in mind, but I didn't know what else to do in the meantime.

A glance in the rear-view mirror, when I returned to the car, suggested a course of action.

"My God," I said to the swollen-eyed, salt-encrusted creature who stared back at me. "No wonder Neptune didn't want you."

I reached under the seat for the envelope that held the emergency cash my mother always told me to keep on hand and counted twenty dollars in one-dollar bills. Then I drove to the nearest convenience store and bought a comb, some cheap makeup, bandages for my assorted small cuts, ribbon to tie back my hair, a tube of liniment for my bruises and stiff muscles, a microwaved sandwich and a cup of blistering hot coffee.

When I stepped out of the store's restroom, I smelled like a pharmacy and looked like a hooker who specialized in the more esoteric forms of satisfaction.

"Listen, honey," said the middle-aged clerk as I pushed open the front door, "you don't have to take that from no man, you know what I mean? You ought to have the son-of-a-bitch arrested."

My answering smile was grim.

"I'll do that," I said, "if it kills me."

I sat in my car in front of the convenience store and thought and planned until eight o'clock. Then I stepped up to the pay phone in front of the store and called the mayor's office.

"I'll put you through," her secretary said cheerfully, only to come back on the line a few seconds later to say in a quite different tone of voice, "I'm sorry, Miss Cain, but the mayor is unavailable to talk right now. Give me your number, and she'll get back to you."

In a blue moon she would; the mayor was getting back at me for my behavior in her office the day before. I said, "Tell her I'm calling to offer a contribution to her reelection campaign."

The next voice I heard was the mayor's.

"Jenny!" she said brightly, all my sins forgiven. "Great to hear from you! What's this about . . ."

"Barbara, I have a question for you."

I asked it.

She answered it.

"Now then, Jenny," she said, "how much are you thinking of contributing to the campaign? I'm sure I don't have to tell you that you'll receive a tax credit of $100 for every . . ."

"Yes, I'll send you a check."

"For how much?" she said bluntly.

I told her and she, sounding surprised, thanked me. She probably thought it was my way of apologizing; or maybe she thought I was trying to buy support for my father. She was wrong on both counts. We hung up, after exchanging brittle but friendly farewells. Well, I thought, I could always contribute twice that amount to her opponent to balance, and tip, the scales.

My single question had turned out to be an expensive one, but not nearly so costly to me as to someone else.

I dug more change out of my pocket. After only a short wait, Jack Fenton came on the line.

"Jenny," he said, "what have you been up to?"

"You've been talking to Barbara?"

"No, Webster. He says . . ."

"I can imagine what he says. Listen, Jack, I'm sorry but I

don't have much time. I desperately need some information that you can provide and I don't have time to get the police to get a court order to do it."

"Jennifer, I won't do anything illegal."

"I'm only going to ask you to do something that you have every legal right to do. And then, once you have certain information, I'm only asking you to give me a simple yes or no answer, nothing else."

"What do you want?" he said, so that I felt like a bad risk for a loan. I was borrowing heavily on his goodwill, and from the sound of his voice, I was nearly to my limit. "Jack, there should be a checking account in your bank under a certain name." I gave him the name. "Would you please look it up and see how it's been used lately?"

"Jennifer, I . . ."

"Wait. Just do that, then you can decide whether to take the next step."

"Which is?" he said forbiddingly.

"You don't have to give me an answer to this, Jack, but *if* you happen to know if the person who holds that checking account has a trust either in your bank or somewhere else, would you, could you also check on the status of that trust? Has it been paying out, and where have those payments been going?"

He didn't say anything.

"Jack? Will you do that?"

"I'll look up the checking account," was all he would say, but that was enough for now. I knew that if he found out what I thought he would find out, he would feel morally obligated to take the next step.

"That's all," I said.

"Call me back in an hour," he said, and hung up. If he didn't get the answers I expected, I was going to lose a friend, an ally and possibly my job.

For the time being, that was all I could hope to accomplish on the phone.

I returned to my warm, dry car. I had an errand to run.

* * *

This time, the police had not only padlocked the front door of Lobster's house, but they had an officer assigned to watch it. He was parked a few unobtrusive yards away in a brown sedan, looking as if he had only stopped long enough to eat a sandwich. But I was willing to bet his coffee break would last all day, until someone came to relieve him and take the next shift. Geof was making sure that no one could get inside the house, including me.

With that route closed to me, I drove back up on the highway, then into the cul-de-sac and parked at lover's leap at a discreet distance behind a red station wagon in which I could see only a man's head; it was bent as if toward another, but invisible, occupant. I got out of my car and closed the door quietly, then walked a long way around toward the fence, as far from their activities as possible.

I looked long at the panorama before me: Lobster's decrepit house, the vandalized windows, the lobster pound, the old man's boat bobbing in the bay; at Webster's new shack, the wrecked and fire-damaged pier, at Goose Shattuck's black Cadillac. And I decided that my theory was fact, not only possible but probable, not merely conjecture, but truth. Now I had only to wait long enough to call Jack Fenton back, and then I would have all my ducks in a row for Geof to try to shoot down. And he would try, for mine was a saddening conclusion; he would demand proof before he made a move. And I would have proof, because by then the coincidences would have piled up until they looked irrefutably like evidence.

Below me, the construction continued unabated, just as the murderer so desperately wanted it to. He was getting that wish, but he wouldn't get all his wishes. I shivered then, suddenly overwhelmed by the magnitude of what I was doing: pinning a murder, more than one murder, on a person, and sentencing him to live forever in the hell inhabited by killers, child molesters and other permanent outcasts from the human race. But if I was right, hell was where he belonged, and was, in fact, already where he lived and made himself most at home. His wickedness was frightening; already it had nearly been the death of me. I shivered again, wanting to get off that hill and out of that place.

I did not know anyone had approached until I felt the hand on my back.

chapter
33

"Be careful, Jenny, don't fall!"

Pete Tower grabbed my arm as I stumbled. The pressure of his hand had not been enough to push me over the edge; it was my own overwrought nerves that propelled me away from that hand and too near the dropoff. I let him pull me back to safety, my heart beating like a piston, my lungs trying to find some air.

"Gee, I'm sorry," he said, his round face pink with embarrassment. "I thought you heard me. I didn't mean to scare you like that. Are you okay?"

"Sure, Pete. Don't know . . . what got into . . . me."

"I saw you walk over here," he said, releasing me. "That's my car over there, that station wagon. But you seemed lost in thought, and you looked kinda, well, sad, so I didn't know whether to interrupt you."

"That was you in the station wagon? Just you?"

He nodded, as if it was perfectly normal to find him on lover's leap by himself in the middle of the week. He said, "I was going over some of our financial records, trying to figure out what to do next."

"Next?"

He seemed to find something very interesting to peer at over my shoulder in the bay. "Uh, Jenny, I'm kind of glad I ran into you like this. I want to thank you."

I looked at him in amazement. "What for?"

"You know when you were at our house yesterday?"

"Oh, Pete, listen, I owe you both an apology."

"No." For once, Pete Tower looked strong, decisive. "Hear me out, Jenny. See, I overheard what you and Betty were saying, and I knew what you were talking about. Heck, Jenny, I've always known my wife's a drunk."

I didn't know what to say. My hands hung at my sides, despite the urge I felt to pat him comfortingly. But Pete bore too much of a resemblance to a chubby rabbit who, if touched, might startle and run.

"I've always known it," he was saying, "but I never had the courage to do anything about it. But, Jenny, she tried to kill herself last night!"

"Oh, Pete."

"It was terrible, I was so scared! She said she'd rather die than stop drinking, and she ran into the bathroom and when I followed her she'd already emptied the whole medicine cabinet in her lap. And I didn't know what to do, Jenny! So I called that suicide center real quick to get their help. And there was the nicest young fellow, Frank Dickens. I'll never forget him; he talked to me, and then I got her to talk to him, and well, we lived through it this time."

"I'm so glad." And so guilty.

"So, you see, I thought I needed her . . ." He flopped his pudgy hands helplessly at his sides. "But she's the one who needs me, Jenny."

"I think so, too."

"So she's going to go to one of those places where you dry out, just as soon as I can get her into it. I want her to be well again, like she was when we were young."

"I know you do."

"And so, well, thank you."

"Pete, please. You heard me, you know I didn't confront

her out of the goodness of my heart. I don't deserve for you to be so nice to me."

"We've all got our problems, Jenny." He looked at me so sympathetically, I felt teary. "Listen, I'm sorry about them kicking you off the committee. I told Betty, I said, we better think this through, it's not Jenny's fault that her dad . . ."

"Thank you. But I doubt that Betty will . . ."

"Betty will do what I tell her to do," her husband said sturdily, and then he grinned sheepishly. "At least until she's well enough to talk back to me. If we're lucky, maybe this time next year, everything will be okay with us again."

"What about the café, Pete?" I gestured toward the bay.

"Oh that," he said dismissively. "That's why I was up here today. Couldn't think about this at El Biggo Taco; couldn't work on it at home because it would make Betty feel bad. So I came up here to kind of, well, look over the lay of the land. See, Betty's always been the one who wanted that French café. Me, I'm happy selling tacos." He looked down at his black suit and starched white shirt as if aware of how ridiculous he looked. Those outfits, I thought, must be Betty's idea. Pete was saying. "But the taco stands pretty much run themselves these days, you know, and I was starting to spend more time at home with Betty . . ."

"I see." Finally, I understood Betty's desperation to keep that café perking right along. She wanted to keep her husband busy on the other side of town, away from her secret.

"Yeah," he was saying, "thought I'd come up here and try to get a handle on what to do with that property, without running into Goose or anybody who'd start asking questions." The glance he threw his prime piece of real estate on the bay was not in the least wistful. He looked back at me, with unexpectedly shrewd eyes. "I don't expect I'll have any trouble finding me a buyer, do you?"

"I don't expect so."

"I'll put Ted on it tomorrow."

"Pete, it's none of my business, but what was Betty doing up here the night she was arrested on that DWI?"

His open face clouded. "Didn't you notice, Jenny? There's a liquor store right there where you turn off the highway. I guess she's been coming up here for years, so nobody would see her at the stores out in our neighborhood."

"I suppose she'd come on down here and park and have a drink or two?"

"Betty?" He looked shocked. "She wouldn't park here without me! We have some mighty nice memories of this place, from when we were in high school together." He realized the implications of his words, turned red, then grinned. Bravely, he said, "Was it still a lovers' lane when you were in school?"

"Yes, but that only lasted another couple of years after I graduated. I guess this place hit its peak in popularity a few years before my time. Then Lobster really began to let it go to seed."

"Sad," Pete said lugubriously. He would have felt a good deal happier had he known that his words went a long way toward reassuring me that his wife was not Lobster's spied-upon party. Even if the old man had fixed his telescope upon Betty, it was unlikely he would have been able to identify her.

"I hope happier days are ahead," I said then, "for both of you."

"You're a nice girl, Jenny." He said it so kindly, I overlooked the chauvinism. "I hope, well, that things work out okay for you, even if your father did . . ."

"My father didn't."

"Okay. Well, thanks again." Pete smiled nervously, then made his escape with a wave of one pudgy hand. "See you!"

"Good-bye," I said gently, and then I thought of something. "Pete!"

He stopped and looked back at me.

"What was the name of that young man at the suicide center who helped you last night?"

"Frank Dickens. Never forget that name."

"But I thought they never gave out their last names. How'd you know his?"

"Oh, I asked for him special," Pete told me. "I know somebody else who called the suicide center one time. I remembered . . . that person . . . talking about how great they are, and I called . . . that person . . . to find out who . . . that person . . . talked to."

"Really? Who is that person?"

"Oh, I couldn't say, Jenny. I mean, it's private."

"I wouldn't ask," I lied, "but I have a cousin who needs help like that, and I'd feel better about recommending Frank Dickens if I knew somebody else he'd helped. If I guess a name, would you shake your head, or nod?"

"Well, I guess that would be okay."

I guessed a name. He nodded.

"Suicidal," I said. "And just happened to tell you about it?"

"Yes, you know we're not close friends, really, but I guess there was a need to tell somebody. It's tough, you know, and maybe there was a sense that I'd understand."

"Yes, well, I'll have my cousin call Frank Dickens." The same cousin who was thinking of bidding for majority ownership of the First.

I watched Pete pull away in his red station wagon. He waved as he rounded the cul-de-sac, and I continued to watch until his brake lights flared at the corner by the liquor store. Then I returned to my own car.

Time to call Jack Fenton.

The banker came on the line immediately.

"Jennifer." His voice was old and cold with shock and sadness but he didn't waste time indulging his feelings. "I have obtained, basically, the information you need. I don't know if it's sufficient to warrant an arrest—your detective friend will have to make that determination—but I do know it's highly suggestive." He paused. "Oh my."

"I know, Jack."

"Well." He forced himself to be brisk. "We have a checking account in . . . that name, but it has been inactive since the second week of February, two years back."

"Has anyone inquired about it?"

"Yes, that same week."

"Who?"

"The person you would expect to ask about it. I am loath to use the name over this phone, Jennifer, I'm sure you understand."

"Yes. What was . . . that person . . . told at that time?"

"That most of the funds in the account had been drawn out earlier in the week, and there was no further activity."

"Have there been subsequent inquiries?"

"Yes, from the same person."

"And?"

"Evidently, our people have reported no activity."

"What about the trust?"

"Well," Jack said, "you were right, of course, there certainly is a trust fund, but we don't have it. You were also right to assume that I might know where it's held. I do. It's in Delaware, and it's a large one, worth quite a lot of money."

"It would have to be."

"Yes," he said sadly. "So it would."

"Did you find out anything more about it, Jack?"

"Yes. I phoned an acquaintance of mine in that trust department and I asked a few questions. I'm sorry to report that every answer seemed to lead to other questions."

"Yes. And?"

"The trust still exists, of course, and it's still paying out regularly to the same person. But the trust received instructions some time ago . . ."

"Excuse me. When?"

"In March of that year."

"Yes, it would be March."

"The trust received instructions to deposit the quarterly checks directly into an account at a bank in Atlanta."

"This can all be done through the mail, Jack?"

"If the signatures are right, yes."

"I see."

"Wait, I'm not through. Once I had that information, Jennifer, I took it one step further and called that Atlanta bank. After all these years, I do have a few contacts across the country. I know more bankers than anybody in his right mind would ever care to know in a lifetime." He laughed shortly, then coughed. "At any rate, I asked my friend . . . uh, the president . . . to simply check the account to see if any withdrawals had been made since it was opened."

"And they have not," I guessed. "Only deposits."

"Correct. It's an interest-bearing money market account, by the way, with check-writing privileges that have never been used."

"It makes sense, doesn't it?"

"I'm afraid so. If the checks from the trust were deposited in this bank, eventually we would notice that no checks were being written on the account. Considering the, uh, circumstances, someone here would most likely call it to my attention, and then the fat would be in the fire. So it had to be another bank, another city."

"Isn't the Atlanta bank curious?"

"Not at all. The account is being used, you see, if only for deposits, and they merely assume it's being used as an investment rather than for check-writing purposes."

"One last question: has anybody besides you asked that trust department in Delaware about the activity of the trust?"

"Oh yes, but they don't personally know the people involved, so they won't give out that information. And, when they received the instructions about where to deposit the checks, they also received strict instructions about maintaining the confidentiality of the account."

"Well," I said.

"Jennifer, you know that all of this could be interpreted in a perfectly innocent manner?"

"Yes. That is the intention. It's meant to look innocent. But we don't believe that, do we, Jack?"

"No," he said reluctantly, "we are not so naive."

"Thank you, Jack."

"These are errands I would rather not have run."

"Would you rather it were never discovered?"

"No!" His voice instantly regained its vigor. "We are dealing with something despicable here and it must be brought to a stop. What will you do with this information, Jenny?"

"Take it to the police."

"Still, there's the question of the body."

"Oh," I said grimly, "I have an answer to that, as well."

"Oh my." Clearly, he was distressed. "Oh my. How is your father, dear?"

"All right, I hope."

"Good. Well, good luck, my dear."

"Bye, Jack."

I put down the phone long enough to look up another number. Thanks to Pete Tower and Jack Fenton, I now had enough ammunition to fire the final, fatal round.

"Hello?" said a familiar voice. How could a killer—one who had tried again only the night before—carry on with daily life so casually, so confidently?

"Hi, it's Jenny Cain."

"Jenny?" There was unmistakable shock in the voice, but it was quickly converted into hearty surprise. "Jenny! What can I do for you?"

"There's something I think the committee—and you in particular—ought to know, and since I'm no longer a member, I thought I'd pass the information along to you."

"That's decent of you. What's up?"

"Do you know the Towers are not going through with their café at the harbor?"

"No. No, I didn't know that."

"Well, I just heard about it from Pete today. You haven't seen him today, have you?"

"No."

"Well, he told me they're canceling all construction . . ."

"What!"

"And they're draining the pound, dumping the architectural plans and putting the whole thing on the market."

"You're kidding! When are they going to do all this?"

"All I know is they're going to raise the gate on the pound

tomorrow and let it drain so it will be ready for dredging; and they left orders for Goose to stop construction today."

"Why, Jenny? Why are they doing this?"

"I wish I knew. But I think the committee ought to know because of the importance that each element of the project has to the whole."

There was a bitter laugh. "Where have I heard *that* before? Well, maybe I'll give Pete a call, see if he won't slow things down until we get a better idea of what's going on."

"I think you're too late," I said quickly. "They were leaving town right after I saw Pete. He left all his instructions with his secretary; she's supposed to be making the calls today to bring everything to a complete standstill. Except the draining and dredging, of course."

There was silence at the other end of the line. I waited, my heart beating in my ears. "I think they must have gone crazy. Well, we'll just have to wait until they get back, I guess. But thanks, Jenny, I'll be sure to pass this on to the others. How's your father?"

"How kind of you to ask." I fought to keep the sarcasm from my voice. "To tell you the truth, I had a little accident last night that prevented me from seeing him."

"I'm sorry to hear that. Are you all right?"

Yes, you son of a bitch. "Yes, I'm fine. No damage."

"Good. I guess your father is keeping away from Liberty Harbor these days, huh?"

Why the emphasis on my father? "Yes."

"You know, the vigilantes have disbanded, now that he is, uh . . . although I'll tell you there's been some talk of calling them out again, since he is, so to speak, on the loose."

You capital-B Bastard. "Oh?" I said.

"But right now, there aren't any guards at the harbor at all. Do you know if the police are watching the place?"

Ah-ha. "No, they are not."

"Not?"

"Not."

"Well, thanks again, Jenny. God bless, and all that."

"Nice talking to you." Go to hell, and all that.

I hung up, gently. Then I placed two more quick calls to ask two big favors. Then I called the police station, but Geof still wasn't in.

"This is Jenny Cain," I said. "Has there been any word about my father?"

"Let me check." There was a murmur of voices, then, "No, I guess not, sorry. Any message for Detective Bushfield?"

This time, I left explicit instructions as to where Geof could find me, and when, and why.

Then I walked down the street to The Buoy for a crab sandwich and a beer. I didn't have to wait long for Geof to show up. At the table for two that I'd taken at the rear of the restaurant, he listened to me for fifteen minutes, questioned me for half an hour, listened for another five minutes, then argued with me for an hour.

Finally, he stood and looked down at me.

"All right." His face was lined with fatigue and worry. "You're right. We'll do it your way."

I reached for his hand. In that noisy, bustling place, we were immobile for a long moment, holding onto each other.

Then he left. I ordered a cup of coffee and settled in for a long wait until dark.

chapter
34

A police sedan was still parked near Lobster McGee's house when I drove past it around nine that evening. From there, I drove around the cul-de-sac, finding only a family who seemed to be picnicking in their car while they looked out over the bay. I decided to park down on the same level as the project, but a good half-mile away, and walk back to it, keeping to the hillside to avoid being seen.

I didn't bother to cover my tracks since it would soon be too dark to see them anyway. I made my way across rocks, sand, grass and dirt to the back side of Lobster's house and crouched beside the back porch. Goose had switched off his floodlamps; objects only a few yards away were turning into vague forms in the growing darkness. I heard, but couldn't see, the water of the bay as it lapped against the sand, the pier, the new docks. In the heavy air, the stench from the lobster pound was nearly overwhelming.

I glanced up at the broken window in Lobster's bedroom. But there was no movement, no telltale flash of metal or light to betray the presence of my witnesses. I could only hope that Geof had already arrived and was hidden from view, along with Ailey and other reinforcements. Witnesses to this final act were imperative. If I were the only one to see it, people might accuse me of inventing it to spare my family.

The rain, which began the night before, had only sporadically ceased that day. Now it began to beat a quicker, harder, more urgent rhythm as if it were in a desperate hurry to end the drought.

Still, no sign from the upstairs window. What if they were delayed? Would I have to face this alone? My heart began to beat, like the rain, a little too fast and hard for comfort.

The sound of feet shuffling through the sand and grass tuned the speed control knob of my heart to a still higher notch. I crouched deeper into the shadows of the old house, and watched.

Someone was advancing toward me, walking close to the cover of the hills, as I had. I couldn't see the face yet, but the person was dressed in slacks and a shirt; it could have been male or female. But when it reached the other side of the pound, its sex was apparent. "It" I had begun to think of the person as "it," as if loath to assign it human status. "It" was no longer deserving of inclusion in the race; it walked outside the boundaries of anybody's standards of decency.

I craned around to peer up at the bedroom window. If there were any witness or protection there, I didn't detect it.

The figure at the edge of the pound didn't waste time. It took off its shoes and laid them on the grass, then rolled up its pants to its knees. Quickly, it walked over to the weir that served as a sluice, letting the ocean and lobsters into the pound when the tide came in, then as the tide moved out, allowing the water through again, but penning the lobsters inside. Below the weir of heavy oak slats was a concrete dam with a gate that could be raised to drain the water.

I glanced back up at the broken window in Lobster's room, feeling as frantic as Betty Tower on her worst days. Still no sign of habitation in that room from which the old man had been pushed—through the window, into the pound—to his death. Was Lobster McGee already dead when he hit the water, or did he drown because he could not swim?

I looked then at the top of lover's leap at the broken fence where Amy Denise Sullivan had been pushed to her death, over the edge, down the sharp rocks, into the water in the pound below. Sweet, neat little Amy Denise. She had loved her unsuccessful real estate salesman husband enough to spend some of her trust fund on a boat for him. But she had hated boating too much to agree to join him in making his dream of retiring at the age of thirty-nine come true. Amy Denise, whose money provided the answer to a failed man's dreams, but who may have made the mistake of saying to him, "We will live on that damned boat over my dead body."

The drumbeat of the rain slid from ragtime into hard rock.

I watched Ted Sullivan raise the old gate to release the water from the pound and drain it. He must have drained it, too, after both of his first murders; perhaps Lobster had watched him drain his wife away as well as kill her. Now he wanted to get a look at the bottom of the pound, the gate, the tunnel, before anybody else did, to make sure there were no remnants of his victims. He would have felt pretty safe by the next spring when the Towers had planned to drain this pound; by then more than two years of tides and saltwater would surely have destroyed any lingering evidence.

Through the rain, I watched him stand beside the pound. He seemed to be looking into his depths. Did he see faces floating before him in his imagination? Did he see the wife he took to lover's leap? Did he see the old lobsterman who would not have been able to identify the murderer until he saw the photograph in the paper that week of the newly elected president of the board of realtors? Then a phone call. An arranged meeting at the old house. A walk to the bedroom to show the realtor how the blackmailer knew what he knew. A demand for money. And then another burst of violence, another human being pushed over an edge, and down . . . into the pound with the lobsters. And then the killer going around the old house, breaking windows, making it look as if vandals had been at work so no one would question a single broken window.

Then early the next morning, donning the old man's slicker, taking the old man's boat out to the traps, making sure of being seen at first, then gaffing the pot to set the stage, then escaping unseen through the rough water in a powered dinghy, perhaps even the one from the *Amy Denise.* And leaving it to the Coast Guard to come to the logical, but wrong, conclusion.

He stood in the rain, staring at the pound.

I crouched in the rain, staring at him, waiting.

Ted . . . identifying Ansen Reich from my fateful description. Tampering with his brakes, meaning only to frighten him, probably intending to follow it up with a warning phone call, but killing him instead . . . so that Reich could not implement his threats to impede the orderly progress of Liberty Harbor where Ted's bodies were buried.

Ted . . . who didn't want the police looking into the reasons why someone might want the harbor to proceed . . . committing harmless acts of arson and vandalism to make his inadvertent murder of Ansen Reich look like part of a scheme of sabotage. But only someone closely connected with the renovation would have known just where to aim his "sabotage" to do the least damage, cause minimum delay.

Ted . . . playing into Hardy's hand, as well, by making the obscene phone calls that implied racist motives, and by using the cross from the Unmarked Grave to commit his next murder.

Ted . . . leading the committee to think on Sunday that Atheneum McGee had agreed to leave us in peace, then stabbing to death the second man who had threatened the realtor's safety and freedom. How surprised Ted would be to discover the link between Ansen and Atheneum, a link that had fascinated the police, but about which the murderer knew nothing.

And Ted . . . the only member of the committee besides Jack Fenton who knew where the *Amy Denise* was anchored and how I was getting back and forth to it. Of course he knew: it was his boat, and he'd asked me to keep him informed of its whereabouts. It was that realization that had come to me as I struggled to survive his attempt on my life the night before.

I could barely see him. There was no way he could see me. But then a flash of lightning illuminated him.

I stood up.

chapter
35

When he saw me, his lips moved, but I didn't wait to hear what he had to say. I leaped onto the porch, as if to confront him.

Suddenly he was dashing toward me in his bare feet. Along the opposite side of the pound he came, around the corner, and now along the side where I was backing away from him through piles of trash and old tools that Lobster had deposited there years before.

This was happening faster than we'd—I'd—anticipated. The desperation and violence of the man were quickly triggered. Instantly, I knew we'd calculated wrong, and the sum of this equation might be my death. Ted could have his hands on me in the fatal few seconds before Geof and Ailey could race from the upstairs bedroom.

He was within feet of me, his mild face twisted into something evil.

One of the tools at my feet was the rusty pitchfork that Lobster—and then the Towers—used to feed fish parts to the soft shedders in the pound. I grabbed it, then stabbed the yard of air that stood between me and the man who'd already killed four people and tried to kill me.

It stopped him in midstride.

He stooped to pick up something I couldn't see, and hurled it at me. Suddenly, I had something foul and slimy in my face. Blindly, I let go of the pitchfork with one hand and wiped frantically at whatever it was that was dripping down me. It was fish parts that he had scooped from a bucket by the pound.

In that moment when I was off balance, Ted flew at me, arms outstretched, oblivious to my weapon. I grabbed it with both hands again and raised it to ward him off, but the slime from the fish parts made my hands and the pitchfork slippery and I couldn't get a purchase on it.

His hands were inches from my face when I dropped the pitchfork and took my only means of escape: once again, into the water, only this time it was the horrible old lobster pound full of filth and shedders.

Ted grabbed the weapon I had dropped and began to stab wildly at me as I struggled in the water. Another flash of lightning illuminated his murderous intent. One prong of the fork sliced at my shoulder and I screamed, letting in a mouthful of putrid, salty water. With that arm numb and disabled, I kicked my feet violently and plunged my other arm up and down, trying to escape that tormenting pitchfork. In the last burst of lightning, I'd finally seen figures at the window of Lobster's bedroom, figures that Ted, with his back turned to them, did not see. Hurry, my mind screamed to those figures in the window. Could they even see what was happening down here in the rain and blackness?

My hair had wrapped around my face, blinding me. Desperately I reached out with both hands in front of me, ignoring the searing pain in the wounded shoulder. One hand touched something smooth and firm.

Ted took final aim at my face. I hauled my good arm out of the water and hurled the only weapon I had. I heard a grunt of surprise from Ted and then a scream of pain and the pitchfork fell harmlessly in the water behind me.

"Get off me!" he screamed as bulky figures appeared to grab him. But it wasn't the police that Ted wanted removed from his person: It was the lobster I had thrown at him and which was now clamped furiously to the hand he'd thrown up to protect himself.

I grabbed the pitchfork and held it out to Ailey Mason so he could grab it and pull me in. Dragging my torn shoulder, I clambered up the side of the pound until I was lying, then kneeling and finally standing on solid ground. Geof's face appeared out of the darkness and he opened his arms to me.

Then he got a whiff of me. And changed his mind.

In the patrol car on the way to the hospital, they made me sit in the back seat and they rolled all the windows down, despite the rain. At the hospital, a nurse, a doctor and two orderlies came running up, only to back off quickly. "You can have this one," said one doctor to the another. "Oh no," said the second doctor, "it's all yours." Finally, they washed out, disinfected and stitched the wound, which was more painful than serious, and then they escorted me to a hospital shower. A nurse's aide handed me a huge, fresh bar of deodorant soap. "Take your time," she said sweetly.

It was difficult to scrub with one wounded wing.

"Don't worry about it," Geof said when he picked me up at the emergency room exit an hour later. "We'll work on it when we get home."

He drove me to the Ramada Inn. We parked in front of Room 106, got out and knocked at the door.

"Jennifer!" my father exclaimed when he opened the door. He was dapper in a mauve smoking-jacket and matching slacks. For once, he looked me straight in the eye. "My dear, I do apologize. A young lad rowed out to the boat yesterday evening and said you had paid him to come tell me to meet you back at the marina. Well, I hauled anchor and sailed off immediately! When you failed to appear, I grew quite concerned, my dear."

I saw tears glistening in the gray eyes.

"But," he said cheerily, "this nice police detective found

me today. He assured me you were all right, and it was all some kind of practical joke. Honestly, the things people find funny these days is simply beyond me."

My father pulled me into the room with him, smiling an apology to Geof, who waited just behind me outside the door.

"My dear," he said quietly, "I know he's just a policeman, but he is a Bushfield, and I think he's interested in you. If he asks you for a date, you might consider going. I wouldn't mind, you know. In fact, a merging of the Cain and Bushfield interests might be an excellent idea."

I peered around my father as if to inspect Geof. "Well," I said doubtfully, "he is cute, but are you sure you want a cop in the family?"

"Jennifer," said my father reprovingly, "don't be a snob."

Past midnight.

"Put down your wine and turn around."

I placed the plastic glass in the corner of the bathtub and wheeled on my bottom so my back faced him, so to speak. Soon I felt a warm, soapy washcloth applied with the expertise of a masseur. He was delicate around the edges of the bandage. After a few moments of heaven, I sighed and leaned fully against his wet chest. Two pairs of knees rose like knobby islands in the water. Geof reached around me with a long arm to retrieve my glass of wine and hand it to me.

We were rehashing the day's and night's events, trying to ease the horror and sorrow out of our unconscious, where they might turn into nightmares, into the light of consciousness where we could try to understand and accept.

"Tell me again," he demanded, "how you knew she had a trust fund."

"It seemed logical," I said. "Ted is the world's worst real estate salesman, but even in his leanest years they lived well. Yet she didn't work outside the home. And still, she was able to give him that boat as an anniversary present. When a woman can do that, the answer is often a trust fund."

"I can't stop thinking about how Ted really gave us the

first clue when we were only kids," Geof said, and I heard pain and regret in his voice. "He was going to retire at thirty-nine, he said, Jack Benny's age. If I'd stopped to add and subtract, I could have figured out that he killed her when he was thirty-two, so that he could have her declared dead, inherit her estate and set sail as he always said he would. That year when he was thirty-two must have been the point of no return: either she would agree to his plans and finance them with her money, or he would kill her so he could do what he wanted to do all along."

"Can you imagine sailing off into the sunset on a boat named after the wife you'd murdered?" I mused, and shivered against him. "You know, when you and I were trying to figure out what might have happened on lover's leap two years ago, we never thought of Ted and Amy. But when I was in the mayor's office day before yesterday, she seemed a little too sympathetic to his business woes. I thought they were having an affair."

"Our mayor?" Geof rested his chin on top of my head and chuckled. "If she ever has an affair, it will be with the head of a Fortune 500 company or a United States senator."

"A Republican senator."

"Yes." He chuckled again and kissed my left ear.

"Well, anyway," I said, wanting to fill in a few blanks left from my revelations to Geof that afternoon in The Buoy, "I called her to ask why Ted had such a tough time two years back. And she reminded me that that was the year Amy disappeared. 'Poor Ted,' she said. He did a fine job of convincing the whole town that he was the loving, suffering husband whose wife had abandoned him for a lover. But he never named the lover. And it was always just his word for it, wasn't it? He even told Pete Tower that he was suicidal over it, but then he made the mistake of giving Pete the complete name of a volunteer he had supposedly contacted at the suicide center."

"So what?"

"So for their own protection, they never give their last names. Ted probably met somebody who worked there, and decided to throw in that little embellishment to prove his misery."

Geof grunted, a sound that reverberated in my spine. "That's typical, Jenny, of how criminals sometimes hang themselves by talking too much. Does them in, more often than not."

I scrunched around so that I could lie on my good shoulder against him and look at his face. "Geof, you didn't want to believe me, did you? In your heart, did you really believe it until you saw him lift that gate?"

"Yes," he said, surprising me. "When I was up in Lobster's bedroom, waiting to see what Ted would do when he realized you had witnessed that incriminating act, I saw something that clinched it for me. Do you remember a pile of newspapers in a corner of that room?"

"Yes."

"Guess whose photograph was circled in bright red in the paper for February twelve?"

"Ted Sullivan, the newly elected president of the board of realtors."

"And Lobster died on the thirteenth, so he must have called Ted immediately and set up the appointment for the next day. And Amy Denise must have died sometime earlier that week. You know," he said then, "it's a good long run from that second-floor bedroom to the pound. We were lucky to get there in time."

"I was lucky," I said humbly.

We soaked until the water cooled. Then we climbed out of the tub, dried each other off and padded into the bedroom. My shoulder was beginning to throb despite the wine, but I didn't want to take a pain pill yet.

Geof reclined on his side of the bed, on top of the covers. I didn't get in beside him right away, but sank onto the floor and lay my head near him on the edge of the mattress. He reached down to stroke my hair.

"You don't have to get on your knees and beg, Jenny."

I looked up to find him smiling. He bent his own face down to mine and kissed me. "At a certain moment tonight," he said, "I will ask you one more time. And if you say no, I will roll over, turn on the light and read this month's *National Geographic.*"

"That's blackmail." I laughed. "And you know where that got Lobster McGee."

"I don't want your money, honey. Just you."

We kissed again. And again. And again. Somehow, I ended up on the bed beside him after all. At a later, appropriate moment, he stopped what he was doing to demand an answer.

"This," I said, "is hardly the time to say no."

We proceeded to merge the Cain and Bushfield interests.

The next day, when the lobster pound was fully drained, the workmen found stuck in the tunnel the remnants of a fat orange life preserver.

epilogue

"You see, Jennifer," crowed Webster Helms. "There was nothing to worry about, nothing at all."

"I wasn't worried, Web."

But he was right: the ribbon-cutting ceremony for the official grand opening of Liberty Harbor was going off perfectly. And he had a right to crow, as did Goose. Web's designs had been translated by the builder into charming buildings. In the ship-building school, the young apprentices were sawing and sanding happily away. The three-story mall rose grandly above the bay, enticing everyone with its mix of shops and pubs. The old pier that Ansen Reich had plunged off was gone now, replaced by a sturdy new one where, already, a few old men and youngsters had cast their lines to see what they could catch.

Across the cleaned and sparkling lobster pound, the old house looked like an advertisement for a paint company. Tourists were lining up to inspect it—not, I suspected, so much for its historical value as a tribute to fishing, but for its titillation value as the site of infamous murders.

Rest easy, Lobster, I thought.

I walked across the new cobblestone path that was designed to look quaintly old, and succeeded, to congratulate
the mayor on this great day for her city.

"Thank you, Jenny," said her Honor, Mary Eberhardt.
"It's a joy to me, personally, to see so many faces of color
among this crowd. I feel that Port Frederick is only beginning to rise, that we will set a standard of racial cooperation
that will . . ."

"Oh my Lord," moaned her husband. "I got me a
politician for a wife."

"It's your own fault, Hardy," Mary said tartly, then
returned his fond smile. "You could have run for the job
yourself, you know."

"I have the Lord's work to do," he said firmly. "And He
keeps me plenty busy."

"Well," I said, "we don't any of us have anything to do for
the moment. What would you say to my treating you to a
congratulatory drink at the café?"

And so we strolled over to the little French café beside the
lobster pound. C'EST LA VIE, said the sign above the door,
announcing both the café's name and its owner's new
philosophy.

We took seats on the open-air veranda, within sight of the
Unmarked Grave that had eventually found a home beside
Lobster McGee's old house. It was, as the Eberhardts had
promised, a simple, discreet, but somehow terribly moving
memorial. We watched a steady stream of visitors approach
it quietly, stand respectfully beside the fence for a few
moments, then move on. An old black woman went down
on one knee and prayed. Her grandchild tossed a home-
gathered bouquet on the grave.

The proprietor of the café appeared at our table, menus in
hand, and observed the scene with us.

"There," said Barbara Schneider, "lies the former mayor
of Port Frederick, Massachusetts."

We broke up laughing, then ordered drinks.

Barbara, more relaxed than I'd ever seen her, personally
returned with them, then sat down at the table with us. Over

her shoulder I saw a poster that advised her patrons to "Vote Republican Next Time."

"Congratulations, Madam Mayor," she said to Mary.

"Congratulations, Madam Mayor," Mary said to her.

"Why aren't you married yet, Jenny?" Barbara asked bluntly.

"Well," I said, "you know, one thing and another."

"Jenny!" all three of them intoned.

The truth was that having finally wormed a commitment out of me, Geof's need had relaxed. "One of these days," we kept promising each other, but somehow something always got in the way.

"Well," Barbara said, "you can have your reception here, if you like. I have just the right appetizers. They're really delicious: lobster hors d'oeuvres. We serve them on a . . ."

She noticed we were staring at her.

"Oh," said the former mayor of Port Frederick. "Well, maybe not lobsters."

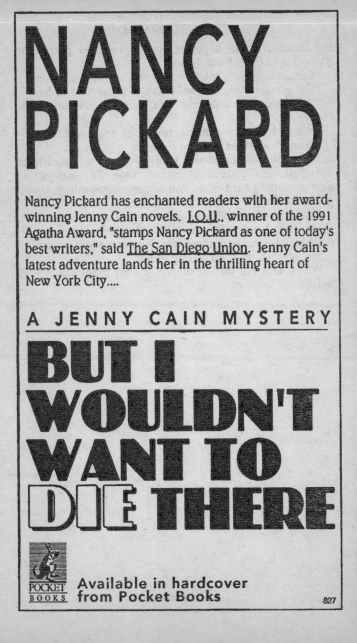

NANCY PICKARD

Nancy Pickard has enchanted readers with her award-winning Jenny Cain novels. I.O.U., winner of the 1991 Agatha Award, "stamps Nancy Pickard as one of today's best writers," said The San Diego Union. Jenny Cain's latest adventure lands her in the thrilling heart of New York City....

A JENNY CAIN MYSTERY

BUT I WOULDN'T WANT TO DIE THERE